For my great-grandmother, Lucy Ellis,
and the innumerable freedman

who fought to claim their piece of where they landed.

Dancing In The
White Sand

CYNTHIA L. MATLOCK

CHAPTER ONE

Lani took a chance on being caught and penalized for peeking. She hid behind a low tree limb observing the different tall weeds ahead. At age thirteen, soon, she'd be prepared for her rite of passage ceremony. Perhaps if she found out things before her turn came, she'd ease through the many hard tests. The elders kept so many secrets about the specific food, dance steps, and clothing choices for the big dance. Her heart thumped loudly as she crept forward.

Two ladies were in a clearing picking plants for the upcoming cleansing preparations. Punishment for finding out what the secret plants were was one thing, but the punishment for being found wandering off into dangerous territory by herself, could be worse.

"Lani, Lani, *sare!*" her mother Toluwani's high-pitched voice screeched behind her.

Lani pivoted just in time to see a group of ladies from her West African village screaming and running her way. Hurry where? Her mother's red and white beaded necklace flopped against her slender neck. Oh no. Her father and five of her brothers were away hunting.

"Moeder, Ma, *ki ni*?" she yelled. What, and who was chasing them?

There was no time for her mother to answer, for a warrior swiftly came into view that she recognized as one of King Damutne's. White facepaint across his forehead indicated his tribe. He led the charge of several pale skinned men with nets and guns running right on his heels.

Oh my, the village chief had warned them about slave raiders snatching people for gold and coins. Everyone was supposed to stay close and look out for each other. Lani bolted toward their village hunting area where the village men would be. It was times like this she wished her legs were longer so she'd be faster. She raced forward with all her might along with other girls and women.

The captors were fast. One by one, they caught the girls or ladies behind her and held them. She heard the girls resisting, kicking, and yelling as she burst out into crazy laughter while jumping over mud puddles. Her mother had told her to stop those laughter outbursts. However, often her emotions got mixed up. She cried at the wrong time and sometimes laughed when nervous or upset. She just couldn't help it.

"*Achee, achee, yara*," Lani screamed and laughed with a shrill sound while hurrying, hoping her father would hear and recognize her painful laughter. Out of all of her father's twenty children and four wives, she was her mother's only girl, and everyone knew her strange laugh.

Her father and the other village men came rushing out from among the green thicket ahead armed with spears and sticks. Dropping wild game, they were ready to fight anybody to save their village. An arrow flew by her right ear. A man gasped painfully loud behind her. Then a gunshot rang out. She ducked and kept running over rocks, through thorny vines, and as tall weeds whipped her in the face *yaw, clang*, and *pow* echoed behind her.

Toluwani quickly caught up with Lani thanks to her thin arms and agile legs. Mother and daughter ran together. Before they could jump over an upcoming creek, a net came down over Lani's face. Her mother turned to help her, pounding the man's head like bread dough. Then another man ran in and held Toluwani.

Lani fell and gulped for air, struggling, kicking, and biting at the man's strong arms that gripped her. Some captors looked like her cousins, while some had pale skin and thin noses. They soon overpowered her. She lay there shaking, wondering why they thought a girl who only helped her mother cook, bead necklaces, or occasionally helped her father catch fish, would be good for free labor.

When she got up a few seconds later, her brown face and arms were covered in dirt and grime. One man wearing more clothes than she'd ever seen on anyone, tied a rope around her hand, then extended the line and tied it to the next girl. The group consisted of about fifteen ladies and girls; some wore wrap dresses, neck beads, and all were barefooted. Most had close-cropped bushy hair, and a few ladies had their hair in braids with white shells dangling on the ends. Pulling back with all their strength, they were still dragged along like animals towards the ocean for two miles.

It was a rainy Thursday in October 1858, and water drizzled over them as they trampled through sticky mud and flat marshy land. Lani was grateful her mother walked in front of her as most families were separated. As she stumbled along in line, it looked like the trees were crying right along with her, dripping water on her shoulders. She sighed angrily.

"*Ki lo fa*?" Lani choked out to her mother. Why?

"*N ko mo.*" Toluwani stared painfully back at her struggling daughter while walking sideways.

Lani knew her mother didn't understand either. The other village mothers had spent many mornings discussing their fear that raiders would capture their children. She swallowed an angry tickle creeping up her throat. It was evening, and they hadn't even eaten yet. Next year she would've been separated from the village for the food and spiritual cleansing to prepare for the biggest event of the year in her community—the community festival—where the neighboring villages came together for dancing, good food, and ceremonies.

Quickly a big black snake slithered across the path in front of them. Lani jumped to the side and looked up. Above them partridge birds flew from tree to tree chirping and seeming to follow the captives marching in a line.

Then suddenly, a flock of birds darted from a dense canopy of trees ahead. A rumbling like powerful thunder pounded through the trees. The lead man stopped and turned back to his other slavecatcher bringing up the rear. When the front man stopped, the whole line became motionless.

Fear spread across his face as he scanned the thicket, cautiously raising his gun. She knew it was a herd of elephants heading to a waterhole. And she silently hoped the elephants would rush towards their line, which would cause the men to panic and give her time to get loose from the rope. Then she'd be free, and she knew plenty of hiding spots.

Within minutes, however, a loud trumpet blasted from the elephants, and slowly the rumbling faded. Lani realized the elephants must've got a whiff of their scent and gone another way. She moaned, held her head down, and started the walk again to the unknown.

Gradually, the salty Atlantic Ocean air drifted their way, and more gray moss draped from the lower trees. When they reached the dark golden sand of the coastline, they found two big ships docked there with their sails flapping in the wind. Open boxes of gold coins and guns lined the port. Strange men with firearms and village leaders from other tribes counted the coins and forced people onto the deck of one ship.

If only her village had better weapons to fight with, then surely, they would've defeated those slave traders. She sighed heavily. They outnumbered the traders thirty to one, but guns versus rocks and fists were not a match.

"Go, wash, feet," said a guard holding a whip. He pointed to their feet, then the ocean. Next he untied her group and followed them to the blue water's edge.

Lani glanced at her mother and the others wondering what language the man was speaking. His words sounded strange. They weaved towards the ocean through tied up grown men and ladies who sat looking shocked with downcast heads. What surprised her most was that next to the edge of the docks were stacks of cocoa beans, piles of palm leaves, and people that were being counted to board the ships. Were they just another item to be carried away from her country and sold somewhere else?

Her stomach felt queasy, and she was weak with disbelief. Did they not know, her village elders had taught them they were a proud and determined people? Her father and village warriors had fought off and won many tribal wars. In fact, if the marauding raiders had not surprised their village, maybe she'd still be home. The massive ocean waves roared in front of them now. Too soon the guard tied her up again.

"Up there. Island ship," the ruff-voice man hollered, pointing to the ship on the left. Several men carried bundles on their shoulders onto the huge vessel.

Lani gritted her teeth, stepping out of the ocean onto the same beach she'd traveled too many times. But then it was to swim and to collect seashells. Her feet were wet, and her heart heavy. She gazed back out over the blue horizon and wondered what other countries were out there, and how far? Then she peered ahead at the palm trees on the coastline, hoping for any sign of her father or older brothers charging out of the woods ready to rescue her and her mother.

She refused to go easily and decided she'd search for freedom or survive long enough to get back to her family. This was not fair. An unexpected capture. Right before completing the important passage dance, and her preparations for womanhood in her tribe.

Immediately, she was forcefully pulled to the ship's loading ramp. That's when she fell on her bottom on purpose, which drew the girl in front of her down. The line of eight women and girls had to stop. A quick guard yanked on their rope, but she deliberately fell flat on the ramp. The guard tripped and started shouting lots of odd words. He stumbled over to cut her rope and dragged her kicking and screaming onto the ship. She was dumped on top of a croaker sack full of coconuts and hit her head. She passed out, and the ship departed, changing her world as it sailed away to an island.

CHAPTER TWO

L ani's head hurt. It'd been six months since she was knocked out on the ship that brought her to this Caribbean island. She still had headaches. She kept her eyes cast down and eased herself onto the soothing warm sand of the beach. Two teacher-guards were coming over to work with her group of ten captive girls. She turned and scanned behind her, admiring the light blue sky, turquoise water, and powder white sand edging the Atlantic Ocean.

"How could this be? A beach like this should be for swimming and relaxing," she muttered and turned around. Evening English classes were about to begin.

Rubbing her forehead, she felt overwhelmed about all these new expectations. Learn English, be ready for a new owner. At least her new friend, Molayo, whom she'd met on the island, sat quietly next to her. Molayo was two years older and from a neighboring village in Africa. They'd immediately bonded over shared village customs and their upsetting capture memories. They patiently waited in the shade of several swaying palm trees.

"Get to your places." Ademola startled her by clapping his large hands for attention in front of them. He tapped a stick against his palm. "You will know basic English before you leave this island. If I fail, it will be painful for both of us." He glared over the girls with a mean gaze.

Her arms quivered, and she scooted closer to the front along with Molayo. Most of the girls, like herself, were afraid of the tall, imposing Ademola. He wore traditional tribal nose rings and carried a large stick. And she'd never seen him blink. If he didn't have on a mud cloth apron with motifs of zigzag lines and fish bones that identified his tribe, he could've passed for one of her distant relatives. She wondered years from now if other men and boys would wear earrings in their tongues, eyebrows, and even ears. She couldn't quite imagine that.

Her stomach felt fluttery since she only remembered some English words for their test today. Glancing back at the white waves cresting and rolling ashore, she still hoped her village warriors were sneaking onto land around the bend to rescue them.

To the left was the busy shipping yard where slave and cargo ships floated in or bounced at the dock. At night, the captives were locked in crude log fences. The back gates were continually being opened and closed with people shifting around. Some coming in, some going out, always in a line. She groaned. Leaning back on her hands, she mulled over her study words.

"I wish this school time meant watching a school of fish cause all these new words are *omugo,* stupid," Lani whispered toward a rigid Molayo, keeping one eye on Ademola.

Thomas, their pale-skin guard, hurried over to work with Ademola.

"Yea," Molayo said without turning or moving an inch. "Just cause our hair is short, doesn't mean we no like ribbons and jewelry." She slightly held up her wrist. "What I'd love ez some seashells to make a bracelet," she said in a low monotone.

"Oh, yea? Guess what me, I mean, I got?" Lani kept her arms still in the sand. Then she stiffly reached into her pocket, pulled out several seashells she'd secretly saved, and showed Molayo.

Molayo glanced down, and her eyes widened, admiring the different shells with ridges and curves. Immediately, she motioned Lani to hide the shells. Lani dropped the seashells and covered them with sand, but felt a tingle all over knowing a heartbroken Molayo would cherish them.

The girls sat real still in four rows with their ages ranging from ten to the late teens. They were divided into three main languages: Mende, Ewe, and Yoruba, with a short time to learn English. Both Molayo and Lani spoke Yoruba. However, everyone had learned sign language and understood a raised stick, a pointed gun, or hand signals that said, 'you had better move.'

Blinking and listening to Ademola work with another group, she glanced around and whispered to the girls on the left and in front of her, "*bawo lowa.*"

One girl on the left responded with a sneer as if Lani shouldn't be speaking to her.

"*Ki ni oruko re*?" Lani spoke louder, smiled, and waited, but she didn't respond. "Well, my name is Lani, and I from the Juna Village," she said in her own language, ignoring the girl's frown.

The girl replied, expressionless, her arms folded, "My name is Fadila, and we lived in the king's hut. My father is next in line to be king." Then she jerked her head away and smoothed the fold on her dress to emphasize the elaborate kente cloth. The once bright red and green colors in rectangular patterns were now dingy since their trip across the big ocean.

Lani smiled at her. She knew by the thickness of the fabric it was quality and costly. But. She turned to cut an eye at Molayo on her right as if to say, 'so what?' Fadila and Lani were about the same age, sitting on the same sand, in a strange land, so Lani figured, Fadila *really* needed to settle down.

With a calm face, Molayo pivoted her head and said, "She did. Her father's one of King Damutne's sons, and if he became the next king, Fadila would've become a princess in her village. Little power, but a princess with the best of treatment expected. Somehow, she was out too far away from home with some other girls and got captured. Before her father and his warriors could rescue her." Molayo looked away because she hated talking about the captures.

Lani slapped her cheek and shifted her legs in the sand. Oh my, perhaps if girls had learned to hunt with their brothers back home, then they would've speared one of those cruel raiders. She cleared her throat.

Busy guards like Thomas with his light-colored stringy hair patrolled the areas around them. People were led and moved around further inland between an eating area, resting area, or privy area in the back. Those men wore clothes covering their legs and arms with boots up to their knees. They had to be sweating in all those clothes. Ademola, however, walked around appearing quite comfortable without a shirt on.

Lani grunted, "They'd have to find a large shirt to cover Ademola's broad arms."

Palm trees flapped and swayed in the wind along the coastline behind them. On her right, grown men peeped through the holding pens near the ledge overlooking the beach. Up front, Thomas raised his hand signaling 'hush time.' With all eyes now on him, he started calling out words like "thank you." Lani focused. Ademola responded in a low baritone voice, "*Ese gan.*" And so they went, back and forth, Thomas, Ademola, and then the girls. "*O da abo*" for "goodbye," and other funny-sounding words were added to their vocabulary daily.

Here she was today on a Friday evening, and her group was being prepared for another home. After a few minutes rest, Ademola and Thomas stepped a few feet away and started calling them up six at a time, with Lani and Fadila in the first group. Her leg started shaking as she stepped up to face Ademola. She tried to keep things under control, as her mother had taught her, yet she started snickering.

The other girls in the group came to her rescue and pinched her, telling her to stop before they all got slapped.

Lani felt some hope glancing at Molayo, slowly mouthing out the new words. The clever Molayo had already completed her rite of passage dance in her village. She wore a dingy green dress with upside-down white triangle patterns on it. Her skin was the color of a kola nut. Lani barely saw all her teeth, since she hardly smiled. Around Molayo's long neck was still an imprint of where she once wore beaded neck rings. The captors had cut them off.

Waiting for directions from Ademola, Lani picked up sand and rubbed it between her thumb and pointing finger as her mother taught her to ease headaches. Even after six months, the only memory she had of the rocking ship to this island was sleeping, waking up with her head pounding, nasty rice soup being poured into her, throwing up, then falling back asleep. She took a deep breath. Even though Toluwani stayed on a different part of the island with the older ladies, she planned to sneak away to talk to her mother soon.

Lani bit her lips to suppress the laughter and trembling. Then she moved slightly behind Fadila, who had started fumbling with something in her pocket.

Fadila had a confident demeanor about her and black eyes that bore into you. She stood tall with her long neck and shoulders erect, arms down, and her head held high. Lani could tell she was used to a more royal treatment.

"What's that in your pocket?" Ademola asked Fadila, holding out his hand for her to give it to him.

Fadila hesitated and quickly took her hand out of her pocket and down to her side. "I'm ready . . . Sir. It's nothing, just some sand," she answered him with crisp words, making direct eye contact.

Ademola stared her down but didn't want to waste time on one girl because he had to move on through about thirty other ladies and girls. Besides, they surely didn't pay him enough to put up with small stuff. He signaled her and the rest of the group forward. Lani wiped her sweaty palms on her dress, relieved he'd let her group go.

Then Lani watched Ademola mark off something on paper and told them to practice all their new words learned, tonight, and that they'd better know them all by tomorrow. Walking to sit back down, she exhaled loudly, feeling confused about being treated and trained like a wild animal.

Next, Ademola called up another group. Molayo was supposed to be in that group, but when she got closer to Ademola, she halted, dropping seashells from her clenched fists. The other girls in her group tried pushing her forward. Stubborn Molayo wouldn't move. Lani observed this with caution because she'd seen this behavior in Molayo before. Her eyes would turn red, and then she'd start moaning. Ademola shouted at Molayo to get up to the front row, or he'd knock her out with his stick.

Arms crossed, Molayo started moaning and muttering Yoruba words louder. Lani jumped up and dove toward her just in time to push her friend down so she was not hit by Ademola's stick. Both girls landed in the dirt. Ademola started swinging and beating whoever stood closest to him. Other girls crowded in to protect each other. Those nearest Ademola got wounded the most. Lani felt the stick strike her back. She grimaced yet kept covering Molayo as they scampered to safety.

Even more girls started getting up to protect those who were getting hit. And Thomas, who'd been letting Ademola handle things, started backing up stumbling, yanking his gun strap off his shoulder. He knew a lot of people now surrounded him, and one thing the captain had told him was: to *never* let them gather into a crowd. Thomas got the gun in position, hating the need to use his one bullet today. Then he pointed the gun in the air and fired.

Ka-pow!

A hush covered the area. The roar of the wind and rolling waves was the only thing that could be heard. The guards from the fenced-in men's area started running frantically through the sand towards them. Lani and her group abruptly halted all motion. She rolled over, feeling panicky.

Thomas pointed the gun at Ademola with a cold glare in his ocean blue eyes. Ademola's neck muscles popped out, as if he knew Thomas wouldn't hesitate to kill him if it meant messing with his commission. They were coworkers, not friends. Lani laid on her side in a fetal position, not sure what to do.

"Ademola, Ademola, enough! We can get more money for the bilingual ones," Thomas said sternly, pointing the gun in circles at the girls, then back at Ademola while the girls helped each other up and tended to their bruises. "You know we can't sell damaged property. Put the stick, down." He raised the rifle to his eye level.

Lani gasped and held her breath. No one spoke. They knew he could shoot all of them. Why did all the men with guns look like Thomas? Ademola had neither a gun nor spear. She trembled all over. The two men stared each other down. Thomas moved in closer. Ademola immediately dropped his stick, raised his hands in surrender, and his nose ring seemed to go up and down as he took in deep breaths. She believed he was probably wondering if it was worse to have Thomas shoot him, or control girls who were about the same age as the daughters he'd left at home. Lani sat up slowly.

"Oh yes," Ademola grumbled. "I am working with boys and men on the next trip. Or maybe I will go back to catching and loading. Or even working in the dirty marble mines." He watched Thomas lower his gun. Then he turned to the students while squeezing the hem of his apron. "Go. Get out of my face, all of you. You'd better know the new words by morning," Ademola directed. Then he marched away, cautiously glancing back over his shoulders at Thomas.

Lani felt dazed about where to go. The other girls slowly stirred, rubbing and inspecting each other's injuries. She shook her head. Did they need all this learning a new way to speak, and getting hit just to get ready for a new home? Word was the demand for sugar required "working people like oxen and donkeys." Plus, she still felt upset she had not completed her dance training and ceremony. Maybe it would've prepared her better for surviving these changes in her new life. Hopefully, she and her mother would find a way to freedom.

How would she be able to complete the steps of her rite of passage? She so wanted off this island.

"These are some '*buru*, evil' folks," she mumbled to herself, then huffed along following behind her group as they went off to eat. Trudging past a fenced-in area of captive boys and men, she recognized one from her community in Africa. His legs were longer now than she remembered, and he had more bulging arm muscles. She felt him watching her walk past them.

She limped over to where people were lined up and handed a tin cup. A broth simmered in the big black pots in front of them. A hungry Lani twisted in pain, as her stomach grumbled for any food. Behind them a high wave rolled ashore, crested with white foam, then rippled out, and a guard yelled, "Healthy is a double profit." She wondered what that meant.

Soon it was sleep time. Out in the dark blue horizon, a ship's lamp lights were flickering as it floated ashore. She tried not to worry about which captives would leave next week from the island. Or who'd stay here and keep chopping away. Survive. Just hold on. Forget the rules that the girls and ladies are kept in a separate area; she'd sneak off and find her mother in the morning.

CHAPTER THREE

The next morning, cooking fire smoke floated upwards as Lani scanned around her. Several older ladies were standing near a water well in the distance. If Ademola caught her too far from her area, she'd be ordered back.

Covering her mouth and refusing to cry, she headed purposely towards the well. Within minutes, she spotted her mother surrounded by several injured and frightened girls who were also looking around, watching for a patrolling guard.

The glow of the sun had just started spreading light, and the clouds received the first benefit that morning. Purple and gold encircled them. The same colors mirrored over the ocean waves. She hurried because after morning corn soup everyone went off to work.

Toluwani stood out among the other slave ladies, for she always held her head high when she walked. This was probably from years of carrying things on her head. She could balance a load of clothes or a bundle of firewood on her head and never drop it. And her skin was as smooth as brown cocoa butter from head to toe.

Lani rushed in among the ladies washing their faces and drinking water from clay pots near a well. A lady with orange rags braided into the ends of her hair nodded at Lani with her eyes blinking. The adult captives had learned slyly how to communicate with few words. They could speak wonders with their eyes or facial expressions. A quick nod of the head or a subtle movement of the eye signaled others to watch it, hold on, I'm with you, or you know better than that. They weren't allowed to gather in groups of more than two or three. Lani blinked hard at the lady and moved closer to her mother.

Miss Toluwani, as the girls called her, was patting the back of an orphaned girl. The short girl was bending away from Lani's mother with a grimace as if she ached all over. Lani bristled and hurried to Toluwani. It was not the right time for her mother to soothe other people; she was not *their* mother.

Lani marched up and roughly pulled the girl back. Then she slid in close to Toluwani showing her the bruises on her arm. A few girls stared at her disgustedly and slowly left for their quick meal. After that they would go to the sugarcane fields to chop or strip ribbon cane.

"*Oponu*! Lani, you know better." A frowning Toluwani scolded her child, then gently pushed the other girls away. "Now, I always make time for you." She pulled Lani over to inspect the bruises on her arms and back.

Lani pursed her lips while her mother cared for her wounds. She hated it when her mother talked to her like a baby in front of others. And even worse, they had to speak English only. She hung her head in shame as she remembered the village rule— we are *all* family. Her father had four wives who all shared a community cooking area. Still, come on, sometimes a person needs one-on-one time. Often she'd talked extra loudly when her father visited their hut back home. Just so he'd know she was in the room.

Her mother pulled tightly on Lani's bandage and she winced. "Sorry, *Moeder*, Ma. When we get to our new home—"

Toluwani put her finger to her mouth for Lani to hush. Then she cleared her throat and became rigid. Tying the third knot in Lani's bandage, her voice became shaky. "Listen, Lani . . . soon we might . . . separate. And me want you to be smart, brave, and make the best of where you may be. Our future . . . but . . . me, I want you feel as secure as possible. And ya, always, always, dream of better days." She stopped tying the knot and gazed out longingly at the palm trees waving in the wind along the beach.

"Ma, please. They've kept us both on this island for over six months. No worry. I've got to study my English." She crossed and uncrossed her legs, wishing her mother would hurry and finish.

Meanwhile, Toluwani ripped a piece off her dress and dipped it in the cold well water. Then she filled a rag with sand and made another mudpack for her daughter's arm bruises. For the life of her, she didn't understand how a human's life could be valued in bags of gold. However, even in April 1859, Toluwani knew smuggling people was big business.

Lani turned restlessly from side to side, checking over the morning crowd. To her right, she spotted Molayo and another girl wandering by and prepared to join them because she wanted to ask about one of those boys in the other pen. There were a few people on the island she remembered from the elaborate community festivals in Africa.

"I be back, Ma. Me feel better," Lani said, shuffling off. If she could get one dance move down, or talk about how to fold the large head wraps, anything from back home, it'd keep her from feeling so homesick.

Picking up more sand, Toluwani added water and pounded it until it became mush when her daughter left. Then she reached for another girl and stood behind her, holding her neck and gently applying the mud. She really wanted to get her hands on some raffia palm branches. And then dye the leaves red or blue and weave all kinds of baskets. Gazing at Lani strolling away, she hoped she'd instilled enough courage into her stubborn child.

Lani bumped into a worker slowly moving to his next area. Most walked like they were in a bad dream. Finally, she caught up with an annoyed Molayo and the other girl who had a broad nose. She asked them a few bothersome questions like, "What is the second step in the passage dance? How can they hide in the forest on the island? Can they get lost on purpose?"

Molayo stopped, put her hands on her broad hips, and rolled her dark eyes at Lani. After a few minutes of walking on, she seemed to realize Lani wasn't going away. So she told Lani to follow her, for she wanted to show her something. Swiftly, Molayo started signaling a few other girls over as well. Since Molayo was well known among the girls as the one who'd completed the big dance, she'd become an automatic leader to the younger girls. Lani admired her confidence, and they became friends real fast.

They all dashed to the privy area. That was the only area the guards let them linger for a few minutes. Lani could hardly wait. Her legs started shaking. She glanced over at Ademola. He appeared busy flipping papers. Further out, Thomas seemed occupied pacing the yard. If either guard caught them practicing an African dance, or playing around too much, they'd be in big trouble.

Seemingly unconcerned, Molayo and two other girls stood behind a line of five girls for cover. She pulled Lani back with her.

"What is it?" Lani felt like her chest was about to burst from excitement. She covered her mouth with both hands to prevent being teased about her buck teeth.

Molayo told her, "Just watch." And then she started a rhythm with her fists and palms like drums, as quietly as possible. They had the cover of the roaring ocean waves to drown out some sounds. Lani tried to ignore the rotten egg smell coming from the outhouse pit nearby and concentrated on the beat. The other two girls picked up the rhythm. Then a dancing Molayo tapped her feet lightly then lifted her right knee, clap, down, lift her left knee, clap, down, then twisted her hips right and then left. Repeat—all to an intoxicating beat.

Soon, the whole cover line of girls couldn't resist the rhythm and started either swaying or bobbing their heads. Lani clasped her head in excitement as she joined in. And oh, her heart beat faster and faster. She envisioned all of them dressed in elaborate yellow or green bird feathers attached to a headband. Then matching red or yellow dresses and, of course, their faces covered in white clay face paint as they'd danced in unison. Rocking and shaking to a drumbeat.

Well, before she could get the twist movements down the lookout girl yelled, "guards!" Ademola came rushing directly their way.

The girls scurried. Lani tried sprinting, but the thick sand tripped her. She fell, rolled, and got back up, hurrying towards the smoking black bean pots. After safely making it to her line up area, she smoothly slid into the back of the line. She took a few deep breaths while glancing up at the sky. Real thankful to escape a lashing this time.

Behind her, Ademola and Thomas had turned and were working with another group of women. Why were these strange people trying to make her into a mindless working girl with no choices? She gazed east then west, wondering where or how she could escape from an island surrounded by water. Surely there was a way such a huge number of captives could surround and defeat the guards?

It was a Friday morning and her mother's sleeping area had lots of movement going on. Lani's eyes batted awake slowly as she peered in that direction. Bewildered, she wondered what could be happening.

"*Moeder*, Ma," Lani whispered, so she wouldn't be noticed moving quickly and quietly like a cat through the morning crowd.

She frantically waved her arms at the line of people leaving the back gate. She knew it was her mother by the way she held her shoulders back. At the ocean's edge, some people were already boarding a big ship along with men loading bags of cargo on their shoulders. Twisting between people standing, some walking sleepily, and some still sleeping on their mats, she had to get to the gate.

As Toluwani followed along in the last group leaving the gate, she checked behind again as she was sure she heard Lani calling her. While searching and hoping to hear her daughter's voice, she was pushed forward towards the ship's ramp. The cloudy morning darkness hindered her vision. Stubbornly, she turned around and sent a beam of love to her daughter. She watched Lani sprinting forward, but a quick guard stopped the running girl at the gate.

"Moeder, wait!" Lani squeaked out as her whole body and throat were so tight. She pushed back hard against the guard at the back gate, balling her fists. They could not leave without her, too.

"We're a pair, I'm with her," she pleaded, holding up two fingers so the guard closing the gate would understand her. A month had passed since the last shipment of slaves was sent away. She'd convinced herself she'd be shipped out with her mother on the next ship leaving the island.

The burly guard flung her over to the side and began tying a rope into a double lock on the wooden gate. Undeterred, Lani ran around him. Then she pounded on the hard gate helplessly as she watched Toluwani's group through the cracks as they were herded up the ship's ramp. The large white masts flapped wildly in the wind, like they were waving at her. Lani knew her mother would want her to be strong like a rock. But how? She leaned into the gate, palms out, and felt the rough wood as she collapsed onto her knees.

There were people all around behind her, and she needed to get up. But first, she ripped off her mudpack and exposed her wounds. To focus on something else and to keep her from biting that guard. Then she stared at her hands and started rubbing the darkened reddish splotches on her arm, which soon began to ache. Harder and harder she hit her arm with her fist in anger until it hurt badly. In pain, her vision became blurry with tears.

An older lady spotted her and pushed back a crowd of orphaned girls coming over for a morning hug. She knew they had to move Lani before she was trampled at the gate. When the lady reached her, she gently pulled her up. Holding her hand, she tugged Lani through the crowd while reminding her of staying in control, how to be a strong young lady, and other things that she didn't hear.

Tenderly, Lani was eased down near the eating area. When a cook brought her a bowl of rice, she threw the rice out, and took several handfuls of sand and tossed it over the rice. Then added more sand and made a big mound of dirt mixed with her tears. Next, she poked two eyes in it. A guard came over and demanded she get up. He stopped in his tracks. Then stood there studying the mound for a minute like it was the most unusual sand art he'd ever seen. Refocusing, he ordered her to follow the group to work.

Lani slugged along in line while grinding her teeth in anger. Yes, she decided, somehow, she'd find out where her mother went.

For weeks, a forceful Molayo and other ladies made her sing village songs, chant prayers, and reminded her of her courage and strength, every day, after Toluwani was shipped out. Despite that, she still felt like her world had ended. She ate very little and even helped strip an extra pile of sugarcane leaves off until her hands were full of small cuts. At least then, she hoped, she'd be exhausted, and maybe could sleep all night. To keep herself going, she remembered her mother had told her, "We are the survivors." Plus, the slave drivers made her keep going with a stick if necessary. Just like nothing in their smuggling business had changed.

That Monday evening after grooming and English class a group of girls, led by teacher Molayo, found her sitting alone staring out at the ocean. They sneaked softly across the sand up behind Lani and started singing a village song:

Ekun yoo gba ibi re woo!

Ra ra yoo dara o yoo dara o, woo!

When they saw a guard staring at them, they immediately sang the same song in English.

"The tiger have a nice meal, look!

No, good luck good luck, look!"

Next, a girl with high cheeks put her arms out and prowled catlike in circles around Lani. Then the girl showed her teeth and made wildcat sounds, *rawrr, rawrr* while pawing at the air.

Molayo flopped down and said to Lani, "That must be a sick cat cause I never heard a tiger sound like that."

Lani held her hand up for them to stop and instantly covered her ears. However, after the third round of the song she knew they would not go away. So, her leg just started bouncing. Before she knew it, she got up and delicately joined in with them. It helped ease her sorrow. However, she missed her mother daily. Somebody was always talking to her about the cane fields, how to run away, school, or reminding her to come get her one-per-day food bowl. She'd overheard someone say, "Americans are surely starting to use sugar and grow cotton." Who cares? She wanted time merely to sit and grieve her mother leaving without her and accept her father probably was defeated back in Africa. She flopped down, winded from singing.

After the other girls wandered away for sleep time, her tired eyes were wide open. She watched the long branches blowing on a palm tree down the coastline. Its trunk bent low out towards the ocean. If she could climb on it, they would both sail away.

Despite her anger about her own losses, Molayo strolled over five minutes later and collapsed down beside Lani. She nudged her in the side. "Sit up. It's not dark yet. We can study together."

An upset Lani didn't move. "I no want to hear no chants today." Her voice sounded heavy. "I'll never complete the dance. *Fimi sile in Yoruba,* or in English . . . just leave. Me. Alone." She rolled over away from Molayo.

"Listen. It's not just the dance. My mother left me with my grandma when I was just two, looking for her a job. I never saw her again. So, my grandma and aunties helped me with the community traditions and social customs, and also, what's taboo. You already know some of them. Things like, no whistling at night in the house, for it might bring snakes inside," Molayo teased and did an 'a heh' fake laugh. Moving white sand around, Molayo patiently scooted closer and bent over her. "There's lots of things you're taught before, during, and after the dance. You never know who you'll meet that will help you. And us." Molayo's voice lowered into a serious tone.

"What?" Lani rolled back over to face her. "That's *irikuri,* crazy." She had never heard Molayo talk this much. She sat up and dug her toes in the sand. There was something about a good foot massage that caused her to relax. Somewhat.

"You can learn the dance steps in your head before you actually do them. Hold up your hand." Molayo grabbed and raised

Lani's reluctant left hand. Then she narrowed her gaze, and with her other hand, started tapping Lani's hand.

"I'm not a baby playing pat-a-cake," Lani said, trying not to smile. She kept her other hand on her mat. "What about when I have my time of the month? How will I learn to cook good food? Who can help us escape here?" She gave unflinching Molayo a blank stare. If she had a spot to run to, she would. How she wished this girl would get out of her face.

"I overheard Ademola say the next ship's going to North America too, as did your mother's ship," she replied, rubbing at her long bare neck.

"Is that far from here?" Lani asked with hope.

"Don't ask me." Molayo dropped both her arms onto her lap, palms up, signaling it was time to play. Now.

Slowly, Lani raised her hands in surrender as the wind blew chilly air across them, cooling her off. In broken English, Molayo started singing and patting Lani's hands. Lani's voice felt forced, yet she participated. Over to her left, she spotted other girls shifting their way. Like a magnet, their hand game soon drew a crowd. As each girl sat down, they pushed the other one over to make a bigger circle.

Gradually, her heart started warming back up. Even Fadila stood at the edge of the group like she might come and join them. Before she came closer, however, she turned and went another way. Soon, a bunch of girls joined in tapping hand-clap games together. Before total darkness covered the island, one girl drew lines in the sand for a hopscotch game. They pulled

Lani up, and she stepped up to the front to show off her skills at this game. She let a little smile spread across her face, then skipped on one leg, two legs, then lifted her hands up to cross the finish line.

The setting sun began to cast a halo of yellow light between the ocean's rolling waves and the dark blue water, and before long it faded to black. Gazing up at the sparkling stars, she couldn't help wondering who she'd meet at her new owner's place. Would she survive the work, find an escape route? Just maybe, she'd reunite with her brother, mother, or someone from her African village area.

CHAPTER FOUR

O n a Tuesday a month later in May, Lani squirmed on a hard-wooden bench and pulled at her dingy brown dress. It was their fifth day on the water. She was in a small cell deep in the hull of a large rocking ship. The island miles behind them now. Long benches lined the sides and back wall of her cell. There was little space in the middle to stand, lie down, shake her thin legs, walk around a few feet, sit back down, or lean back and attempt to sleep. That was all. Until the deck break.

She grabbed her stomach to keep from throwing up. The dank air reeked with the stench of musty, sweaty bodies, and human waste. Little fresh wind blew through the small window up behind them. She felt so helpless and wanted to scream out loud. Across the hall, she could hear grown men in another cell groaning and yelling. Chains were rattling as they moved around. A hallway separated two cells on either side. At the end of the hall were steps leading to the upper deck.

"Please move over, Molayo," Lani said, elbowing a preoccupied Molayo sitting next to her playing with her fingers. Then she wiggled her bottom for more space on the bench.

"Where? Stand and shake. Or lay on the sticky floor," her island friend responded dryly, barely moving her mouth. Then she frowned at Lani strangely with cold black eyes, pursed her thick lips, and started rocking back and forth.

Standing up, Lani quickly grabbed a wooden bar on the side of the large locked door in front of them, bracing herself from falling as the ship swayed side to side. She stroked her chin as she looked around at her fourteen fellow cellmates. The female captives ranged in age from twelve to forty and were in their own world of what-ifs and what's next.

"I can't believe this. Only a month after Ma's ship left," she said to Molayo. "After rice soup, the next thing Ademola and Thomas had said was 'follow them this way.' I knew something was different when Ademola counted us twice and then led us toward the ocean. Before work . . ." Lani choked on her tears.

"Yea, I can hardly breathe. And we're packed in this rocking cell, like fish," Molayo grumbled, pulling at her thick coiled hair.

"I'm wondering what's worse, my back pain, or the hard feeling in my chest? I feel like a heavy wet blanket's wrapped around me," Lani added, then she wiped and pinched her small nose. "And it stinks in here. Smells like a hill of cow mess."

The room was otherwise eerily quiet with only a few mumbles and groans heard. Lani squinted up at the little light filtering through the deck door above. Then she heard a loud bass voice down the hall yell out. "*Binu asiwere!*" My goodness, *a guard just got called a 'sorry fool' in Yoruba.*

Suddenly, a big wave hit the ship. Lani clenched the bar tighter, holding on. "I wonder if I'll ever see my mother or father again? These people are *irikuri*, crazy." She glanced around. No one answered or said a word to her. She drooped her shoulders and sat down when the ship sailed more smoothly. Closing her eyes and blocking out her dim view, she visualized the island they'd sailed away from. The white sand caressed her feet, the palm trees waved in the wind, and best of all, the sky was filled with cotton-like clouds above that she wished she could climb on and float away. A sudden jolt from the ship slowing down an hour later brought her back to reality. She rolled her neck and shoulders to relax while wondering what slave work she'd have to do. She was about to be sold in a strange land, to new people.

The dark hull flooded with the new morning sunlight. As they waited for their door to be opened, Lani started biting her fingernails. She hoped she would not begin laughing as she listened to keys a 'rattling in their door. When a slim guard opened her thick wooden door, she squinted and strained to see what lay beyond.

"Come on out, hurry up," the guard yelled while unlocking another door. He adjusted the gun on his shoulder strap.

The first captive man at the front of the line tried climbing the steps. He shook and kicked his legs bound at the ankle with chains. With only one deck break in six hours, all of them had painful, cramped muscles, not to mention the seasickness.

Restless, Molayo pushed Lani, which caused her to push the lady in front of her. Like dominoes, the line moved forward up onto the deck. When her group finally lined up at the railing, another line of mumbling shaking captives formed behind them.

Lani gasped, utterly shocked at the shoreline and how murky brown the water looked. Grayish sand edged the ocean. What had happened? It was the same ocean, but now had dirty brown water. No palm trees?

She spotted Ademola lining up the next group and couldn't hold back her questions. "Ademola, Sir, where are we?"

He lurched towards her with a frown on his face, and his left hand raised. "Stop asking questions. Texas gulf. Now turn around."

Lani leaned away, prepared for his fist. Swallowing hard as Ademola walked away, she slowly straightened up and watched other big ships, small ships, fishing boats, and cargo boats pulling in or floating out from the dock near them. Raunchy fishy smells surrounded them as white seagulls squawked above. She jerked to the side and so wanted to ask what part of this country Texas was located in. Mainly she wanted to know if her mother was sold and bought in the same area.

Then out of nowhere, she started smiling and snickering to herself. An elderly lady behind her with strong legs kicked her slightly in the ankle and gave her a stand-straight-and-behave look. Sporadically, Lani kept giggling as she stared straight ahead waiting for the guard's next direction.

Behind her, she heard chains rattling as the last group of male slaves came up on deck. Suddenly, one guard hollered, "Stop!" Before his fellow guards could get the locks back on one released man's ankles, the freed slave raced to the rail. The muscular man wearing only an apron leaped into the water. The captain jumped up on his big box ringing a bell and yelling, "All hands-on-deck, all hands prepare . . . money lost . . . overboard!"

Guards charged up from the hull below. Down from the masts above. And every corner of the ship. They frantically got their weapons, searching all around for placement. Direction. There were lots of other vessels docked at this busy port. One determined guard dived into the water swimming after the man splashing away towards land further down the coast. The other male slaves, still in shackles, started pulling each other by their ankle chains trying to run. Instantly surrounded by guards, they stopped with their neck muscles tight.

Lani ducked down, trembling. "For sure, oh . . . If I can get the right angle, I'll dive overboard and swim somewhere too." They did not know she knew how to swim. Unlike some of the village fathers, her father encouraged her to be a tough girl. She loved to help her father catch fish underwater back home. Now, gazing over the endless ocean, nothing looked familiar. Even still, she reached up, gripping the rail, ready.

"Down. *Be'ko*, no! They'll catch you," Molayo commanded desperately, grabbing and pulling on Lani's other arm tightly.

Lani yanked her hand loose, gazing out over the horizon with her insides jumping for the runaway man to go, go. Hesitantly she bent down, telling herself she must hold on. Where would she go? Maybe someone would help her later?

Then the captain rang the bell one more time, and all movement on the ship ceased. Water splashed wildly in the ocean as the slave swam farther and farther away. The guards were posed to shoot, but with so many boats coming in and going out they did not fire their guns. Finally, the pursuing exhausted guard gave up and started waving for help. They signaled him back and threw him something to float on back to the ship.

In the meantime, the other guards had gotten things back under control on board. The ship's captain stood in a broad stance. Two guards stood beside him with pointed guns scanning over the crowd in case someone else tried to bolt, run, or fight. The guard's faces were stone-like.

Slowly, Lani's heart rate settled down as they herded her over near water buckets at the back of the deck. Pouting, she wondered where the escaped man had gone? And wished she too had somewhere to run. Seagulls glided and dipped above their ship several minutes later, squeaking and squawking. She waited and watched as one came in for a perfect landing on the rail beside her.

"You see those birds? What if one day someone invents a machine where people can fly through the sky?" Lani turned to Molayo and whispered. Then she paused and glanced around cautiously.

One guard coming their way turned to gather wash buckets.

Clutching her sides, Molayo bobbed her head in agreement watching the birds also, and then said, "Now hush." She held up a hand, palm facing out to Lani. "We've seen grown men trying to walk in unison with chained partners, and ladies' dignity exposed for all to see, and you want to talk about, birds and flying." She folded her arms, and her left leg started shaking, then her whole body trembled.

Lani knew not to say much more. Pinching her lips, she pulled at the back of her thick hair. She knew Molayo was the only one from her family who'd survived the raid. The girls waited in silence for several minutes and watched the flapping birds flying above them. Somebody said they had to get cleaned up for the next event.

A slave auction. How was she supposed to make it through a sale? A few guards started passing them buckets filled with soapy water. Each girl was given a rag to wipe their face and wherever else they chose to clean themselves. The guards had to keep bringing fresh buckets of water. It felt so freeing for Lani and the girls to splash water and feel that their hands and faces were clean again.

Unbelievable. Lani felt like one minute she'd been helping her mother put holes in seashells for necklaces. And now she was sitting here wiping her face, looking around, and wondering who could take a girl from her home without permission, all before she'd completed her passage to adulthood dance. How could they expect her to work for them? And how could they send her mother away on a different ship?

Lani dipped her rag into the bathwater again and pondered who'd buy her. And she sure wished, at least, they'd have some decent food.

CHAPTER FIVE

The girls finished washing all over as the midmorning heat began to warm and dry them. Fadila started a snickering, and Lani felt relieved that somebody else had started a burst of laughter. Pretty soon about five other girls along with Lani began squeezing their mouths to hold in laughter, wiping their eyes, and throwing water at each other. She wanted to slow down time before they had to get off this ship and her freedom is completely gone.

The guards' shirts and pants were getting wet from removing and replacing the wash buckets as they tried not to slip. After a few minutes, the guards yelled and threw rags at them to "dry up and stop it," and the group gradually settled down. The exhausted girls flopped down drying their arms, legs, and the tears which had formed somewhere between the heavy laughter and sadness.

Next, the guards came over and dropped baskets filled with dresses in front of them. Lani got up expectantly and then groaned after picking through a basket of dingy white cotton dresses. When she put on an ugly dress, she looked down and grumbled. "Well, they have one-size-fits-all for everyone." Since she was shorter than Molayo, her dress reached her ankles. She raised her arms out in disbelief. "No, fair. Now I have to go around dressed like a grandma?"

After looking around, she also observed disappointment on the ladies' faces. Probably because they remembered how they'd carefully dyed their own cloth with clay, rocks, or crushed insects to create unique colors. If only she could find the right bug to squeeze and add some color to her dress. Soon noises of the city and shipping port became louder. Paddlewheels swished through the water. Folks ran behind wagons. People whistled and yelled, "What a catch, fresh fish," and it echoed across the dock.

Her head started hurting, and she did a hand massage to calm down. Thomas marched deliberately towards her corner of the ship. While she tried not to think about going out into the crowded city ahead of them.

"Hey. Line up, time to get off." Thomas's voice caused her to jump. He directed the girls to the ramp while telling another guard, "Texas is selling $6 an acre land grants. And that's what I'm going to buy next."

Lani frowned and got in line. "Where you guess we go from here?" she said softly to the older lady with braids standing in front of her shaking her head.

"Child, God controls, and is always with us," the lady said with her right fist raised to the sky to assure the girls surrounding her, and probably herself, too.

The ship's masts flapped even harder in the high ocean winds as the captives followed a guard off the exit ramp. On the street, Thomas and Ademola stood on either side for the final inspection. Each girl was inspected and passed forward. When Ademola got to Fadila in front of Lani, she held both hands in tight fists. He reached for her hand. Fadila abruptly leaned back and put something into her mouth. She swallowed hard, almost gagging.

"Come here. What'd you swallow?" Ademola shouted with his face twisted in anger. He snatched Fadila over to him and pried her hand open.

Fadila held back tears as he squeezed open her slender fingers. In her palms were two polished reddish quartz rocks. She'd held onto them for the whole trip, to remind her of Africa.

Lani did a low fist pump. "Alright, Fadila," she grinned. "A girl can save something." Then she swiftly became poker-faced while Thomas padded her down. When he finished, he signaled her forward.

Ademola jerked the remaining rocks from Fadila's hand, put them in his pocket, and pushed her over with the group. He clenched his teeth while looking at Thomas. Then he examined the shiny stones.

"I promise you, this is my last trip. I have decided my next job *will be* working in the dusty African marble mines," he informed Thomas.

Lani wished there was a way she could go back with Ademola. Unfortunately, another guard with slick black hair and frown lines on his forehead pointed her forward. Too soon, fear crept back up her neck and she was scared of what this new city and country would hold. While she slowly followed the others out into the busy streets, her heart began racing to a triple beat.

Two and three-story wooden buildings lined the hardened dirt streets. Some had porches attached to them, while others had swinging doors with people going in and out. The road felt warm to her bare feet. Her thin eyebrows raised when she observed how many more pale-white people were in the city compared to brown ones. She'd never seen this many white people in her life. Folk's skin tones ranged from blue-black to pale-white as they hurried throughout the crowded streets, mingling with animals and wagons.

Lani and ten others from her ship marched in a straight line behind the lean, wiry guard. So many new sights. It felt like she was suddenly lifted and dropped into another wild dream. She clutched her chest as she gazed over the crowd, and the girl behind her bumped into her back. A lot of ladies wore long sleeve white tops with collars covering their neck, long flowing dresses with wide belts, and head bonnets or big hats. In May? *This country must be very cold.* The ladies were dressed entirely from head to toe. On top of that, some of the men had on tall black hats with long coats down to their knees. How she dreaded the notion of a real winter. How would she find enough covering? In her country, it was either a rainy season or a dry season, but never cold.

"Ugh . . ." A hard poke in the side with a fist caused her to bend over in agony.

"Stop your daydreaming. Keep up." The evil-eyed guard stared at her like she had no chances left to hold up the line or she'd regret it. The others waited, staring straight ahead.

Lani coughed, held her side, and hobbled forward. The need to hit something or someone just about overwhelmed her, but she kept up with the group.

Flatbed wagons loaded with people rolled through the dusty streets as the horses dropped poop everywhere. She bit her bottom lip. For the first time, she became more aware of her skin color. Most of the people driving wagons, leading captives, or coming out of the buildings were white people. She looked down at her brown arms, sighed, and stepped high, being really careful of what she stepped over.

Up ahead, a group of captives followed another man down the same street. Her temples throbbed. Could it be, maybe? One of the ladies was petite and slender and walked with short steps. Lani stared at her in hope. But when the lady turned around, she felt so alone again and dropped her head. It was not her *moeder*, Toluwani. Keeping up, she dabbed at her eyes while almost bumping into a man cutting through their line. Then she skipped to catch up with the group.

To the left, a more massive crowd gathered as they moved into an open court area. Folks shouted and talked among themselves, and she strained to understand bits and pieces of what they said.

Given it was May, green grass and small white flowers bloomed beside the buildings. They were led past a crowd up the front to a platform that had steps leading up to it. A sign dangled above it, and she heard someone yell, "Here's the slave auction." Her chest felt like it had a rope tightened around her. Now, what are they going to do with me?

One at a time, she watched people from her ship going up onto the platform. It looked like a cattle auction. A slave went up, then a man called out numbers and pointed to people lifting their hands in the crowd. Sold! Then the slave went down the steps on the other side. Next.

While her line waited to mount the platform, she noticed two men staring at her group. One was richly dressed with a gold watch hanging from his vest, and the other one with faded tan pants held up by suspenders. Their faces were almost identical. They had to be twins.

In front of Lani, Fadila circled her head left then right. How many times back on the island did she tell people her father would get enough money together and send for her? Lani wanted to tell her to– forget that.

When it was almost time for Fadila to mount the steps, she held her hands out like she was about to climb a stage like a princess. Then when a guard told her to move up, she started wobbling like she was dizzy.

"Steady now." Lani stepped up, balanced Fadila from behind and whispered, "Did you know my grandpa presented me with dried fish bones as a gift during my naming ceremony? What these auction people don't know is, in our village, a person's name has a meaning. Remember at the naming ceremonies, seven meaningful things are gently rubbed against the baby's lips, like honey, pepper, and palm oil?"

Fadila straightened up and nodded. Then said, "Yes, they did, for me too." Then she locked her back into a perfect pose.

"*Be'ni*, or yes," Lani continued while watching the guards who seemed preoccupied. "The dried fish stands for the child will find its way, no matter how rough life or the waters get," she said, crossing her arms. She hoped that memory would help them both mount the stage and calm her quivering stomach.

Next, Fadila pulled at her dress, squared her shoulders, and mounted the steps.

A shock wave went through Lani immediately, because she heard Molayo start moaning behind her. Two girls were between them, yet Molayo's piercing sound rang throughout their area.

Oh, no. "Molayo is about to blow up," Lani said and dreaded what could happen. She'd seen her meltdowns before. After her eyes turn bloodshot red, she'd shake, and whoever was closest to her would get hurt. Lani glanced back. Luckily, a lady started massaging Molayo's stiff shoulders to calm her down and hold on.

Before she could turn back around to check on Molayo, a guard pushed Lani from behind up onto the platform. A bearded man with brown teeth told the waiting crowd, "This is a good buy. Knows English well, quick to learn, long years of service . . ."

Lani felt terrified, and her body tensed. The guard raised her left, then her right arm. Uncontrollably, her thin nostrils flared, and she wanted to blast the man with a mighty sneeze. She gazed out over the crowd staring at her like hungry lions watching a piece of meat dangling from a tree. When the man put his hand in her mouth to check for sores and if all of her teeth were in good condition, she counted backward from three. *If he holds his finger in my mouth one more second, I'll bite down with all my upper, and lower teeth, and pull a plug out of his finger. That'll make him say, "ahhh!"*

After he removed his finger, she continued to breathe deeply as the bidding went on. She distanced her thoughts from what was happening around her. She thought about diving into soothing ocean water and chasing a zillion silver or yellow striped fish towards her father's net. Her father would swiftly say to her, "No weak girl acts, come on, get it together."

Sold! Aghh! Immediately, Lani felt the man push her abruptly forward and told her to follow a Mr. Jack Tate.

CHAPTER SIX

As the evening sun started its descent, four slaves followed Mr. Tate from the auction. They included a muscular teenage boy, Lani, a full-grown man, and a lady in her mid-thirties wearing a white head rag. They trudged along in line with a confused Lani. She couldn't believe that they could be going to yet another ship. Ahead, the street ended at a smaller shipping dock. People passed them coming back from the docks with bundles and empty wagons.

They paraded by several groups of sluggish workers walking behind armed men. She avoided eye contact with the humiliated and embarrassed looking brown people shuffling along in lines like children. Forcing one foot in front of the other and proceeding with her head tilted down, she felt her stomach boil with anger.

"*Je ki a sa lo,*" the stout, slave man whispered over her to the fidgety boy in front of her. The boy slowed his pace, which caused her to slow down, too.

Lani flinched because she knew he had said, "Let's run away." *Wait . . . which way?* She slowed her steps, which created a gap between her and the boy. The boy stopped and checked behind him, with panic on his face. That created a wider space between himself and Mr. Tate who'd kept marching, leading them through the crowded street.

Her arms tightened as they all crept backward in a row. Two steps back, then three. Oh no. Suddenly, Mr. Tate stopped, backed up, and spun around like someone behind him just yanked hard on his ear. The captives stopped in their tracks. He unhooked the knife hook on his belt and marched back to them. Lani wobbled, with her heart pounding so hard she started getting a sharp pain in her head.

"Keep up with me. No talking. And don't try me," Mr. Tate stated loud and clear, with his jaw muscle twitching as his blue eyes bore into each of them. He pointed the long-legged boy forward to the waiting shipyard, and then he walked more beside them this time.

Lani began feeling lightheaded from holding her breath and shaking so. She stumbled back a step, inhaled, then skipped forward to keep up. If they had made it to another street, maybe she would've seen which way Molayo and Fadila went.

There was no time to say goodbye to anyone or see which direction they went. Just like that, her new friend and old friends were gone. She felt totally alone. Her chin quivered as she held in a whimper. It felt like an ocean full of tears were rolling back and forth inside of her, waiting to spill out. Then she wondered if she'd ever make new friends again. Just forget about learning the dance, she told herself.

The auctioneer's voice faded in the background. "A strong worker, broad shoulders, fine buck. Do I have 800, yep 850, yep 875?"

Mr. Tate's twin brother with the black vest and dark hair had raised his hand again and again and taken everyone in Lani's ship group, except her. She'd watched Mr. Tate stare at his wealthier-dressed brother like he was upset, because he'd continuously outbid him.

Control, hold it; Toluwani would've been proud of her for trying to keep it together. Her new owner dusted his felt hat against his pants, and she noticed his weathered sunburned skin with frown lines cutting all across his forehead. Finally, they stopped at the smaller shipyard, down several blocks from the bigger ships.

Lani smacked her lips, tasting a bitter taste in her mouth. She soon realized it was blood from where she'd repeatedly been biting her inner lips. Patting her mouth, she watched men load several small paddleboats while Mr. Tate pulled wooden boxes from a wagon nearby. Two large black pipes towered way above the boats. Gray smoke began puffing out of the pipes.

Beside them was the busy port with people at stands selling different red and yellow fruits, leafy greens, and bread loaves. It reminded her of the market back home. One captive marched by wearing a faded black dress with jagged white line drawings still visible on the bottom. Lani lightly touched her throat. Oh, how she wanted that design on her dress right now. For she knew the zig zags meant 'life is not a straight path.' Today she felt at the bottom of the zig and hoped one day she would go up with the zag part.

An older man moved the ropes in front of the boat allowing people to board. Mr. Tate told them to wait there until he spoke with his overseer. A man ran towards their boat waving his hand. Promptly, Mr. Tate stepped out to meet him with his eyebrows furrowed.

"Where you been, Ace?"

"I was coming. Uh, those are the new workers?" He pointed at Lani and the other three. Then he turned back to Tate. "Don't worry about me. I'm no coffee boiler," he said, wiping his mouth and talking loudly. The man with straw-colored hair and deeply tanned skin appeared younger than Mr. Tate and was tall and slender, whereas Mr. Tate was shorter and more round-shaped.

Mr. Tate shook his head disgustedly, picked up his trunk, and boarded the paddleboat. Lani clasped her hands in front of her, then dropped them to her side, wondering about these two men. The others stood by waiting awkwardly.

Next, Ace signaled them to follow him. He led them to the back deck of the boat which had a cabin for passengers, and a smaller room above for the captain. Several benches and chairs were on the back deck. Best of all, there was more space to walk around.

"Yes, this is a much better boat compared to my last two ships," she muttered under her breath.

Behind the chairs were stacks of crates loaded with cloth, large croaker sacks, and then more passenger's wooden trunks. She shifted her feet uncomfortably, wanting to sit down, except Ace hadn't told them to sit. So she just stood there feeling lost while he moved sacks around behind them.

Ace finally turned around and came towards them with his arms swinging. He talked loudly, like they were hard of hearing. "I'm Massa Ace, uh, yo overseer," he said, prancing around them in circles and inspecting them up and down. He stopped in front of Lani and grunted.

She tried holding her breath. Whew, his breath stank. It smelled like he'd been eating sour weeds.

Gradually, Ace backed away from them and stood with his feet spread out wide and addressed them slowly, "I'll be here, there, and everywhere. So, don't get no ideas." He glared at them, then pointed them to their chairs.

Lani ground her teeth and focused on which chair she'd sit in. The older lady swiftly sat down so she sat next to her. She listened to the sound of the water lapping against the boat still tied to the dock. Then she studied the planks on the ship's deck as they bounced, wondering where the boat would stop. Did Mr. Tate grow sugarcane, too?

Counting the lines on the deck floor, she almost missed Mr. Tate coming back out of the cabin door. He strolled over to Ace standing by the rail in front of her seat. He held a tin cup.

Ace tapped Tate's shoulder. "Now listen, Tate, I'm hunkey dorey." He pointed to the workers. "Feels like this gonna be a tough year, since cotton buyers are getting picky. Glad we got more help." He seemed to study Mr. Tate's reactions.

Mr. Tate slowly nodded. "Yep. We need a good cotton crop. And this may be the last shipment of slaves we can get. Why they've already started war cloud meetings about ending slavery." He rubbed the back of his thick neck and watched a passenger board.

Lani stared at the cabin door, hoping they wouldn't catch her straining to hear them. End slavery? She blinked rapidly.

"Unbelievable, boss." Ace threw up his hands. "They want to change our way of life? Uh, have us starve? How we gonna make it without free labor? I've got a family to feed." He stomped off to the back railing.

She noticed Mr. Tate's cheeks turn a rosy color. Wow! It was the first time she had seen anyone change color. What did that mean? Her new owner finally became aware of her being near. He glanced over at his workers and went back inside. Lani dropped her eyes.

When she gazed back at Ace, he scanned her and then looked away, shaking his head. Slowly he strolled around to the other side and joined a few people watching the boat fill up with passengers. Lani hooked her fingers together, squeezing them hard to hold off a crazy laugh. Several smaller boats loaded with bundles of cargo bobbed and bounced in the water next to them. She glanced sideways at the boy sitting a couple of chairs over and suddenly remembered his face. He was at last year's community festival back in Africa. She wanted to ask him to check, but they weren't permitted to speak. He wore loose pants and kept rubbing bruises around his ankles, completely ignoring her. She remained quiet.

If this man only knew he had bought the wrong girl. For she knew how to swim, cut up the wild game with her father, and run through a rainforest. She rocked nervously side to side in her seat. *Oh, let's get this boat moving, please.*

CHAPTER SEVEN

A strong wind blew as gray birds waddled around dropping mushy deposits and eating scraps from the fishing boats. Suddenly, the boat's whistle blasted their ears with a loud sound. Lani flinched and twitched in fear. Her fellow workers all flinched too, searching the skyline. It was dusk dark. Gradually a humming vibration began. Her leg started shaking. Where or which way could she swim from here?

Staring up at the captain's room above them, a man fiddled with wheels and knobs while black smoke puffed from the boat's pipes and filled the sky. Then the paddle wheel on the side turned, and water gushed over the wheel. They gradually floated away from the pier as Lani and her fellow captives sat back, hushed in uncertainty.

The boat pushed through the choppy waves of the big ocean to a much narrower, calmer passageway or river. Within an hour, at eight-thirty, it was black dark. Cold, damp air hovered over her and the other deck mates. Lani only wore a thin cotton dress and had no shoes. So she started shivering. She reached for the piece-a quilt behind her and pulled it up to her neck. Her arms began breaking out in little goosebumps from both the cold night air and searching the riverbanks for what may lurk in the dark woods.

She knew step one of the rite of passage was to be separated from your past. But who could imagine her separation would be from her whole village and family?

Soon they were floating through the eerie fog lingering around the boat. It seemed the night creatures felt safer with their sharp night vision. Frogs croaked, crickets screeched, and hooting and howling echoed around every bend. Lani clutched the quilt tighter and still trembled.

The captain's large lamps provided some light as they floated out of the fog. She checked behind her and noticed her Watcher, Ace, had come back out to his seat and fallen asleep. Close to him a heavier-looking quilt lay unused, covering some items near him.

"This a *sele* or scary river. It's freezing. I'm getting us more cover," she said to the stiff lady next to her. How could the lady sit so long without moving an inch?

The lady shook her head, signaling no and for Lani to sit down. The man and boy grunted to warn her too that no, it was too dangerous. Lani quietly got up anyway. Like a lioness creeping up to her prey, she glided towards the thicker quilt. Ace's head was tilted way back, and he snored loudly. It was a chance she chose to take. Being the only girl in her family back home, she'd always had to prove her bravery to her brothers. The slave man shook his head and pointed to her seat. Unstoppable, she moved forward.

Reaching for the quilt, she discovered it covered bolts of cloth. Gently, she tugged it, and Ace turned in his sleep. She stopped. Her mind raced, wondering what she'd do if he woke up. Smoothly, she gradually inched the cover into her arms. Oh no, one end was under his chair. A quick yank would do it. She jerked the quilt, and his chair rocked—a mistake.

Ace's eyes flew open. "What the . . . Gal, are you crazy?" he squealed, shaking his head and batting his sleepy eyes. Then he sat up, reaching for something to throw at her. "That quilt is for the cloth and seeds. Get back in your seat." His hands flared, searching, and he picked up his coffee cup.

She hurriedly tiptoed backward to her seat and dropped down just as a tin cup hit the back of the head. Another cup flew over her, splashing into the water. She scooted way down in case the angry man or a board hit her next. Staying down, she grabbed her wrist and dug her fingernails into her skin holding on to be quiet. *Don't laugh or move.* When she glanced around her, she noted that all four frightened captives had scooted down lower in their seats. After holding her breath a few more seconds, she cautiously rose back up to peek at Ace. Thankfully, he'd shifted in his chair, dropped his head back, and gone back to sleep.

One by one, they sat back up. The lady was a 'huffing, and the young men were mumbling, "*irikuri,* crazy girl." Forget them.

She'd overheard them whispering ideas since their chains were taken off of how they could easily overpower Ace. They both appeared strong, and she figured they could pick her up with one hand.

She glanced towards the lady while keeping her head down. Then she inched her chair closer to her and massaged the back of her throbbing head. Together, Lani and the lady wrapped themselves under the same thin quilt. Body heat would have to do for now. Lani's breathing slowed as she concentrated on the rocking boat and the smooth churning of the water swishing over the paddlewheel. Finally, she fell asleep.

Her eyes jerked open the following morning when she was startled again by a morning whistle. That whistle! Someone yelled, "Anahuac." She stretched and peered ahead with the morning sun glowing behind her. Horses and buggies with big wheels were loaded down with white bales, crates, and people waiting for their boat to dock at the port. Goodness, she was glad because she badly needed to get off for an outhouse break instead of using their bucket on board.

Ace followed her there and back, and when she returned, people were moving and lifting crates and trunks around. Mr. Tate brought them some corn pone. Still barely awake, her stomach rumbled, and she welcomed any food. While she gulped down her corn, she watched him join Ace by the rail beside her. Both men sipped steaming coffee. A wonderful roasted coffee bean smell floated across the deck.

Mr. Tate leaned against the rail. "There's lots of traffic today on the Trinity River, isn't there? This is the largest river basin in Texas which begins and ends in Texas. A General Alfonso de Leon was searching for an outpost of St. Louis, two days before the feast of the Most Holy Trinity, and discovered the Trinity River."

A drowsy-looking Ace slurped his coffee, then yawned widely. "Is that right?"

"Yep. We're almost in Anahuac," Mr. Tate said, scanning the water. "Why that's where the first shot of the Texas Revolution was fired in 1836." He talked in a precise and commanding rhythm, which allowed for few interruptions.

She licked her cup and grimaced, wondering what on earth a revolution was.

"You're full of history this morning." Ace said. "I watched things last night. I'm just glad Texas is a good place for me to take care of my family." He held his head way back, draining his coffee cup, then fingered the stubble on his chin.

Tate put his cup down and then stood back confidently. "And you know what? Mexico wanted to increase its military presence in Texas. Even prohibited further imports of slaves. We need cotton pickers. So, a fight began in Anahuac. That's like the British who tried to command the United States from across the ocean. Let Texas handle its own business."

The teenage slave boy gazed over at Lani and seemed to ask, "Why are they standing over us talking, and why don't they move?"

Neither of them spoke. She shrugged and returned to watching the people on the riverbank ahead. Listening.

Ace raised his deep voice. "I'll tell you what, Tate. I'm too old. Still now, if need be, I'll join any army to fight for our rights." He pounded his chest. "Do you know some slaves have run off to Mexico for freedom?"

Mr. Tate's forehead scrunched up. "Mexico? All this fertile land along the Trinity and Neches river bottoms, and the British are buying more cotton and American goods? We must stop that, because we need *more* laborers. This time I bought extra seeds and supplies back, for a profitable year," he replied, fanning his hand over Lani's area and other crates in the corner.

Lani's ears perked up. Freedom? Now that was a word she knew and wished for. "Mexico, huh?" Most of what Mr. Tate talked about seemed nonsense to her. So, she got up and went to their assigned water bucket, drank some water, and squinted, looking out as far as possible beyond the Anahuac port. How far-off was Mexico? If she only knew how deep Trinity River was.

New passengers got on, and others got off. Two hours later, the paddlewheel turned, and they moved again. Before long, she was lulled to sleep while considering swimming away; but to where? She also worried and speculated about the place they would soon call home.

On a Thursday morning it surprised her in broad daylight. She'd planned on being ready for the next boat whistle. The uncertainty of her journey kept her jumping. Someone shouted, "Port of Cincinnati." People on the banks ahead eased wagons and supplies closer to the loading docks. Maybe this was her stop. If she took off running, how far could she get before Ace caught her? She checked behind her as he started counting crates, making notes, and watching them. His boss joined him, running his hands over the crocker sacks. With both of them out there, she sat back.

"Everything in order, Ace? So many people are getting on and off. Folks will chisel you." Tate began sliding crates around with his stomach hanging over his pants.

Ace stopped counting and put his pencil down on a wooden barrel. Then he cocked his head towards Tate with the wind blowing his stringy hair.

"Huntsville's about fifteen miles over there. It's home of the state clinker. Some guys are in there for life," Tate said, standing and panting.

"Yea, and I know some that need be in there if that President James Buchanan would finally take a stand on slavery." He threw his hands up. "Who's going to tend the crops and help our ladies wash clothes and cook on those woodstoves?" Ace stared at Tate. Then he folded his arms and paced around in a circle.

Wow, these two masters are acting like two village chiefs back home, arguing over territory, Lani thought. Curious, she stopped watching the people moving around on the banks, angled her chair, and focused on her two bosses. She pretended to clean her fingernails. Maybe she'd hear about local routes or the layout of the villages along this river.

"I agree, Ace." Mr. Tate signaled Ace to calm down. "Listen, we've got corn, goobers, timber, and plenty of other things to make it. Cotton's king, yeah. Still, I don't want either of my sons going off to war. This country should work out a way to peaceably allow state's rights. It's one thing to fight the British for our rights, but fighting each other on the same land?" He put his hand on his hip like the idea was ridiculous.

Ace stepped up a bit closer, towering over Mr. Tate. He balanced himself when the boat came to a stop. Then he pulled his black pants up and pointed at Tate's face. "If your deadbeat, cowardly son were tougher, he'd be glad to fight. Why he's told me he's okay with the slaves, 'jumping the broom.' And he knows the state doesn't recognize a slave's marriage. What's wrong with him?" Ace asked, raising his eyebrows.

Tate's face turned red as he ran his hand across his balding head. She knew now that showed he'd become very *binu*, or angry. Tate pushed Ace's finger back and stepped closer. "You don't talk about my boys, or my wife. I left one running the plantation, and he's doing a fine job. Just be glad I still let you work. Cause you, your wife, *and* your two sons might be picking cotton your own trifling selves . . . and it'll be somewhere *else* this fall." Tate's shoulders rose. He clenched his fists as two men rushed over to separate them.

Seconds before getting knocked over by the other men, Lani and the other captives hurriedly scooted their chairs back. She was jammed against the slave lady while leaning back away from all the wild commotion.

Lanky Ace leaned as far backward as possible over the side railing to avoid Tate swinging at him, as the other men held Tate back. The upset man resisted and kept flaring his arms wildly in the air, trying to reach Ace.

Oh, how Lani wanted to stand and get a better view. She rubbed her hands together on her lap. Yes this was getting good, like a village fight between two boys back home. Usually, the boys would have been showing off for some girl. Someone would yell "fight," and everybody would drop everything and run to see the action.

How she hoped the stouter man would do it. *Hit Ace! Choke him now*! She was ready for a tussle, because if they were distracted, maybe she'd have time to plan how to get off this boat.

More frantic men came out to help drag Tate back. He finally shouted to the men to "let me go." Then he pulled his suspenders out in a popping motion, taking wide steps back. Ace straightened up slowly with his eyes bucked in fear. He flashed Lani a mad expression while swallowing hard. She quickly looked away. Then he slid further up the rail, squeezing it, and mumbling.

While chewing on her lip, she slid her chair back in place, completely turning around seconds before a fuming Mr. Tate stomped by her. She pretended to adjust her dress.

Mr. Tate puffed loudly going back inside. Then abruptly, he stuck his head back out the door and announced to them, "And, ya'll going to learn about a 'pass,' when we get there." Then he slammed the door.

She looked at the big burly slave man for an explanation of what Mr. Tate meant by that. The man nodded at her slowly, then opened his left palm and started pounding it with his right fist. Lani grabbed both her elbows and rocked. She searched her racing mind for another remedy her mother had taught her for pain. Then she reached up and slowly massaged her temples, because she sure felt a headache coming on. What were the new people at the upcoming place like? She longed for someone there her age.

Goodness! She could only imagine what type of situation lay ahead if both her bosses fought and disagreed.

CHAPTER EIGHT

After the third day of rocking in tired silence, Lani wanted badly to speak in Yoruba with the lady. It felt like her tongue twisted up differently when she spoke English. But why risk getting hit for talking? She peered ahead as they swayed and dipped along the winding river avoiding sand mounds and jagged tree stumps. Tall unfamiliar trees with needle-like leaves at the top slowly came into view. Surely they were close. She bit her fingernails.

"My . . . those trees and red dirt," Lani whispered hopefully, pointing ahead. She and the lady looked forward in amazement. Could there be coconut trees nearby?

The boat glided smoothly around the next bend with more tall trees lining the riverbank like a thick curtain. The wind blew across the river, keeping them cool on an otherwise hot June afternoon. Slowly, a flatboat drifted past them loaded with cargo. A passenger standing in the back yelled, "East Texas got the best pine trees in the state." Lani groaned, although she had to agree they were pretty trees. And there were droves of them.

Ahead, an animal seemed to be watching their boat approaching. When their churning boat got closer, she saw it was a big brown dog. The watchdog started furiously barking from the riverbank's edge. Then it ran along, keeping up with the paddle-wheel and showing all of its teeth, making sure the passengers knew– this was his territory.

Hurry, please. Lani's muscles tensed as she leaned away from the dog. The captain steered the boat painfully slow past the growling dog. Once they'd passed the danger zone, she exhaled and looked back as the dog's barking faded behind them. "Goodness, if I try'n swim, then run into the thick forest, how would I avoid a dog chasing me?" she muttered, tapping her foot to calm down. She started repeating a chant from back home to settle her nerves. *Agbara*, strength now.

Quietly, they drifted past the backyards of more white farm-houses and faded red barns out among the trees. Ever since they had boarded the boat, the two captive men had ignored her and only talked among themselves. Occasionally, she caught the younger fellow watching her, and he kept squirming and rubbing his ankles. She'd heard him tell the man his name was Agibe, and the man said his name was Osaze. That was all she knew about them. *Bonk, bonk!* Lani snapped out of her escape ideas an hour later as Ace yelled something behind her.

"Finally. We're close to home. Magnolia Landing," he announced, leaning way out over the railing like he wanted to jump.

Home? She took in several quick breaths and massaged her neck, looking around.

When the boat came to a stop, Ace started anxiously running to the back, wildly pushing crates and supplies to the boat's edge. She nudged the lady who sat next to her as motionless as a wooden chair. The rigid lady put her long fingers on her thighs, then dropped her head, with her feet flat and spread apart like she'd made up her mind. When Lani felt the lady lean forward as if she'd decided to run, instantly she scooted up and hooked her arms into the lady's arms. They'd both go together.

But she'd already seen this was a large country compared to the island they had sailed from. Remembering the farm dogs, broad rivers, and unfamiliar land, Lani reasoned there'd be more chances to escape, later on.

"*Ra ra*, no. My dress too long. Not now," she whispered desperately to the lady, pulling back tightly on her arm. The lady was strong and pulled the other way. Lani held on. Gradually, the lady's body relaxed, and they sat back together waiting. One then another passenger began lifting their bags and leaving the boat.

About five minutes later, the cabin door opened, and Mr. Tate came out carrying a trunk. Lani turned and watched Ace shyly smile at Mr. Tate. He dropped a crate and hurried over to him.

"I'm sorry about yisttidy, Tate. I's out of line. Somehow, we'll make it through. War or no war," he said apologetically, reaching out for a handshake.

"We Texans need each other. We may disagree, but we're connected as citizens of this country." Mr. Tate hesitatingly put his trunk down and shook Ace's hand. "My son may be right. The cotton gin was invented to help the planters. Who knows? One day machines may handle the process from planting to picking the cotton. Let's get our things and head home," Tate ordered, stepping off the boat.

"Yep. I've sure missed my family," Ace grinned, leaning his head to one side like he thought Tate was just about silly. Then he turned sideways, angled towards the workers with his legs spread apart and announced loudly. "I'll be over early tomorrow morning and get the workers busy." He signaled Lani and the others what items to carry off the boat.

Lani got up painfully, picked up a bundle of cloth, and followed the hurrying man into the shipping port. This port was a much busier one with larger steamships bringing passengers in, along with smaller flat bottom boats loaded down with cotton bales and croaker sacks. The afternoon sun had folks running and peddling drinks and stuff in baskets. Some were hollering "peanuts, peanuts, fresh bread," while holding their baskets and mingling among the passengers.

Up near a waiting station was small, fancy black houses on wheels hooked behind horses. A man announced, "stage-coaches here." Well-dressed white ladies and gentlemen got into them. Lani wished she could ride in one too because it probably would be a smoother ride.

Following Mr. Tate on wobbly legs, they marched out to a horse stable. They waited as he retrieved his flatbed wagon hitched behind two tan horses with what looked like white socks around their hoofs. After all those days and nights of bouncing and rocking on the water, she felt some relief she could finally get off, and stay off, a boat.

Holding in a scream of unbelief as they loaded up, she heaved herself up and dropped down on a sack of dried corn like a rock. Mr. Tate climbed up front onto the driver's bench.

Then they traveled through the countryside across wooden bridges and rolling hills on a winding dirt road. Magnolia trees with white blooms stood out among the tall pine trees. Her head bounced side to side as the wooden wheels hit rocks and potholes. Raising her hand, she shielded as much flying dust as possible from getting into her stinging eyes.

Upon a hill, she spotted the top of a large white house and braced herself for Tate to turn onto the road on the left ahead. Long rows of green plants dotted the land leading from the house to the roadway. The fields were full of workers bending, or some standing, watching them pass. Surprisingly, Mr. Tate kept the wagon rolling past that huge plantation.

After another hour, he yelled back to them, "We're almost there." He whipped the horses' backs, and they trotted onto a lane which then opened into a clearing.

Seconds later, Tate muttered, "Whoa," and pulled back on the reins. The horses halted in front of a white frame house with a porch covering the full length of the house, a reddish chimney on the side, and two large windows on both sides of the front door. A couple of rocking chairs were on the porch's right corner. Behind the main house on the south side were five unpainted grayish shacks with toddlers out playing in the dirt.

A forest of tall trees edged the backyard. There was an animal stable on the north side with bridles and harnesses hanging from hooks. Farther out in a side pasture, curious, reddish cows raised their heads while chewing on grass that hung from their mouths.

Lani ached from the boat rides and the hard no-cushion wagon seats. So she continued sitting while stretching her sore legs, allowing them to function again.

Hurriedly, two grown men, one more dark brown skinned than the other one, wearing tattered pants and barefooted, headed towards them. One took the reins from Mr. Tate while the other one began unloading the cargo.

Painfully, she got out of the wagon, stretched and looked around, and just stood there. Thank goodness, she spotted some other teenagers. Two teenage girls were standing around a black pot with a fire under it. She watched them pull up clothes and push them back down into water with a long stick. Thick gray smoke floated up in the air. Scanning right, she observed workers plowing dirt and chopping at the ground.

"Well, is this where the boat rides have taken me?" she groaned and reluctantly moved out of the way for the men to unload the sacks.

A slender slave lady wearing a faded white apron approached them. She had a dirty, beige rag tied around her bushy hair. Mr. Tate signaled the middle-aged lady to come over. Lani grunted and wondered if the lady knew anything about large headwraps in ruby red or yellow. Because she sure favored someone from her village, and if she were from Africa, she would've probably preferred a prettier headwrap.

"This here's Martha," Mr. Tate said directly to Lani, grabbing a small bag from the wagon and went around the house.

Lani gazed at the waiting lady. Remembering her African upbringing for respecting elders, she bowed and knew to put an honorific term in front of her name. She'd call her, Miss Martha. Before Lani could move, Miss Martha stepped closer to her with a warm smile. Lani stood there awkwardly stiff as the lady reached over and hugged her. Unsure of how to respond, she kept her hands down at her sides.

Even still, the friendly lady squeezed her and told Lani to follow her. Lani raised her hand to signal to her to wait a minute. So many new surroundings and people in just a few days was a lot to absorb. Over to her right, a man threw feed to animals in a creek bed. What were they? Baby hippopotami? Another young man shouted, "Leave the hogs and come on!" Hogs? People dropped tools and baskets and came towards the front porch for an evening meeting. Miss Martha turned around when Lani didn't follow her. Lani crossed her arms, feeling completely stuck and confused.

"Come," Miss Martha said, signaling with her hand. A questioning expression crossed her face. "What language?"

"Yoruba, now a English," Lani responded, and Miss Martha's brown eyes lit up.

"*Wa? E ka bo*," She gestured to all the people gathering at the big house. "Lawd'a mercy. Yousa not alone, wez together."

Lani's mouth dropped in amazement. "Ese Yoruba, too? Hold on." She wrapped her arms across her stomach and chuckled uncontrollably. A burst of piercing laughter came forth from way, way down in her stomach. Like an erupting volcano, her eyes started watering. She felt it from her toes to her chest and started shaking with laughter. At first, she bent over in laughter. Then she fell on the ground with uncontainable laughter.

The lady's plea for the upset girl to hold it together went nowhere. To save them both embarrassment, Miss Martha stood in front of Lani and pretended to laugh too as she told her to "get up off the ground." But by that time, Lani had lost all control and pounded the ground with her fists for all the evil, the losses, the torture, *and* nasty food. Water spit out of her mouth, eyes, and she held her legs together to prevent an accident.

After utterly exhausting herself, she sat up, wiped her eyes, and dusted the dirt off her dress. With her head held high, she strolled over to the meeting. A group of teenagers stared at her holding their mouths– trying hard not to burst out in laughter.

She did not care. She avoided looking at them and stepped behind a tall man. Inside, she felt so much better.

Scooting in closer to the group, she listened to Mr. Tate standing upon the front porch. He said he'd be fair if everyone gave an honest day's work. She frowned a bit, confused about the word "honest." Like being in the room with a bunch of new people, she wasn't sure what to do, so she gazed straight ahead, feeling eyes still watching her.

Then a woman with long, blonde hair that flowed down her back opened the screen door and came outside. She wore a wide-skirted dress, propped a rifle next to a pole, dropped two obviously dead birds onto the porch, and stood next to him. It was the first time Lani had seen a lady carrying a weapon.

Mr. Tate glanced down at the birds, smiled approvingly at the lady and continued, "This is my wife, Giruth. One of our sons is away at college in Waco, and the other one's gone to town. There's some rules you need to know. If you try'n run-off," he paused and got louder, "you will get caught and beat. Or if the patty patrol or slave patrollers catch you, you could be hung in a tree. You need a 'pass' signed by my family, if *we* want you to leave this plantation. Without the pass, you're subject to up to twenty-five lashes with the bullwhip." He stopped and glared at everyone, although most avoided eye contact with him.

Bullwhip? Lani scratched at her ankle with her other big toe. Slowly, she glanced around, hoping someone would explain. Surely, he was stretching the truth. Her arms started twitching. She felt powerless at what sounded like unfair, *alekokoro,* crazy talk.

"Oh yea, the house," he pointed to the large front door. "You're forbidden. Don't come inside without permission. And never through the front door. Back to work. Y'all already know this." He picked up the birds and went inside. His wife followed with the front door slamming behind them.

About twenty workers with slumped shoulders trudged wordlessly back to what they were doing. A few small children scampered across the yard. Lani stood there stunned until Miss Martha gestured her over.

Since it was late in the evening, Miss Martha led her to where she would stay. They went down a trail to where the slave quarters were and approached a one-room clapboard shack. Inside, the soft dirt floor had six crude, stuffed pallets along the walls. She immediately noticed the outside light filtering through the holes in the ceiling and walls. A wood-burning heater was in the middle of the room. There were a couple of coal oil lamps on a table, and three chairs. That was all.

"You can sleep there. You'll meet the others soon," Miss Martha said, pointing to a pallet in the back.

Lani swallowed hard, realizing this was her new home. Agibe and the older man followed a gray-haired man to a shack. And the lady from her boat was in a shack across the path. Lani stumbled over, dropped to her knees, then flopped face down onto the pallet.

Even when darkness shaded the windows, sleep evaded her. She felt her sore, achy muscles as she lay on the unknown, scratchy bed with a lonely heart. She tossed and turned and felt like rocks were on her chest. She turned towards the wall as Miss Martha, two other girls, and two young boys all silently came in and went straight to their pallets for sleep.

Remembering how the ocean's waves rolled ashore, both back home and on the island, finally helped her float into a deep sleep. Temporarily, she shut out the fear of meeting new people, and unknown work, both, which awaited her tomorrow.

CHAPTER NINE

Lani jolted awake early the next morning. When she sat up, it felt like she was in the middle of a nightmare. It seemed like she'd just laid down. The next thing, someone stood over her shaking her and saying, "Wez got to get out there early."

Blinking hard, she looked around to check where she was but it was still too dark outside. One oil lantern shed a little light over the dimly lit cabin. Putting her feet on the dirt floor, she felt somewhere between groggy and angry. So, this would be her first day on Tate's homeplace.

Propping her elbows on her knees, she gazed at the flickering lantern. Then she focused on the other empty pallets in the room and her new roommates. The houses were occupied based on space, not families. Two young boys of about age eight years old, Sam'l and Wil'm, were already stretching and scratching. Wil'm, who sat across from her, stared at her like she was a new puppy– so she flashed him a grin.

Two other girls of about fourteen to fifteen introduced them-selves. Lettie Mae was square shaped with a few curves and sweet round eyes. Whereas the other one, Margie, had almond shell brown skin, was tall, and thin-built. Both girls were yawn-ing and pulling cotton dresses over their heads. "Hurry," they shouted to Lani. She wiped circles around her eyes, pulled herself up, and stumbled outside.

A bowl of oats was handed to her as the morning sun peeked through, spreading a golden glow across the yard. The work-ers moved around a long table outside near the back of the big house. Roosters crowed, all perched on a fence post near the crib. To the left she heard the jingle of mules' halters being put on. Overseer Ace marched over a couple of minutes later and told her and the other new workers to follow him. It was renam-ing day. What's that, she wondered with a nervous patter start-ing in her chest. She chewed her oats and rose slowly from the ground.

They went to the side of the house where Mr. Tate stood by a table. Ace plopped down in a chair and started taking notes on paper. Lani waited before them, shifting from one foot to the other. She couldn't believe she'd be given a new name.

Mr. Tate gazed at her bare feet, then up at her frightened face. "What was your name over there?" he asked her quickly.

Utterly surprised, she touched her mouth uncertain how to answer. She slowly tilted her head towards Miss Martha stand-ing nearby. Her new cabin mother gave her a go-ahead nod.

"Um, Lani, sir," she said, clasping her hand and watching him glance at Ace then back at her.

"Sounds like Lucy to me. Lucy, it is. Next."

Lani stepped forward and scanned her surroundings. No festivities, just pull a name out of the air. She tugged at the back of her hair and headed towards the wash area. Miss Martha caught up with her and told her to hold out her hand. She stopped, glanced at her, and hesitatingly reached out her open palm. Swiftly, Miss Martha sprinkled salt into it, then gently patted Lani's back, smiled, and kept going.

Lani gasped loudly and let a small smile creep through. She shouted out to Miss Martha, "*E dupe*, thank you."

The calm lady turned back and waved her away as if it was nothing. Some young ladies around the wash pot stared at her. She stood there smiling and forgot to cover her mouth. Oh well, until someone invented a wire to straighten her buck teeth, she'd keep on grinning. For they may not know, salt at a naming ceremony meant the child's life wouldn't be ordinary but filled with flavor, substance, and they'd preserve all that was good. A warm feeling spread over her chest as she painstakingly licked the salt up, one grain at a time. She was now Lucy.

Walking on, her mind turned over the dangers and traps to watch for after listening to them talking last night in her cabin. Would she get lost if she wandered off too far? At the tub she reached for a rub board from one girl. Picked up a wet shirt, and scrubbed it back and forth.

Lani propped up on her pallet on a Wednesday a week later, still tired from pulling grass yesterday. She scooted to the edge, and her whole body locked up from the soreness of using new muscles yesterday. Her other cabin mates were yawning, scratching, and moving around slowly. Immobile, she wondered if someone had arranged a stack of logs around her. Each day started before sunup with a quick bowl of rice or oats. After that it was non-stop lifting, pushing, scrubbing, and chopping work. She helped slop the hogs, shuck corn, haul water, and forgot about sitting down.

After about ten minutes, she finally pushed herself outside. She sniffed twice. A smoky smell of sizzling meat floated across the yard. Picking up a tin plate, she joined the others already eating their oatmeal and smoked hog meat. One girl of about fifteen with pale brown skin, a thin nose, and hazel eyes came over to her and smiled. Then she instructed her, when she finished eating, to follow her to the wash pot over by the creek. Lani hesitated a second before continuing to chew. There were too many bosses around here.

As she looked around the farmyard, she wondered why the other female workers let their bushy hair grow out. She'd have to figure out how to manage her thick hair which curled and grew upward, or she'd have to find something to cover it with. What she'd really like to do was crop it all off.

Once she'd finished eating, she noticed the giant pile of dirty britches, dresses, and bed coverings waiting for them. Five girls were already hauling water from the creek or working on different parts of the wash cycle out in the clearing near the back fence. Two large washtubs were on a stand. And nearby, a big black pot had steam rising from the hot boiling water inside. A simmering fire glowed underneath it. Pulling a brown rag from her pocket, Lani tightened it around her head, went near a tub, and stood uncomfortably straight.

"We'll be working with the rinse water over there," the same bossy girl said to Lani. Then she flipped one of her wavy, sandy-colored pigtails back behind her shoulder and stared at Lani a few seconds. After a quick pivot, she picked up a load of clothes in a bucket on the ground, strolled over and dumped them into the rinse water.

Lani hesitated because the smoke had shifted in the wind's direction and blew right up her nose. She coughed and followed the girl to the first washtub.

"Dip the clothes up and down, and then we'll twist the water out." She demonstrated by moving the clothes around in the water. "My name is Sarah," she announced, watching Lani for a response.

Well, I'm Lani . . . or now, Lucy," Lani said slowly, trying to absorb it in her memory. And she hoped she'd remember to answer to it, instead of looking around for someone else.

"You'll get used to it. Soon it'll be Sunday. And after prayer and worship, we get to go to the fandanga in the evening. Something to look forward to around this unfair place." Sarah looked behind her. "Ooh, there's a lot of singing and dancing." Sarah flashed her teeth, smiling and bopping to imaginary music. Ignoring the fact Lani wasn't talking much, she pulled up another shirt.

"Fandanga? What type of dancing?" Lani asked in a dry tone, surprised and glad she'd finally found her voice. The mention of dancing made her perk up with hope.

"Oh, just rocking, clapping, and singing. We get dressed up, too," Sarah said, swaying side to side.

Lani grunted and kicked at the dirt with her toes. Then she grabbed the other end of a pair of britches or pants. They twisted the pants in opposite directions, squeezing the water out. All of a sudden, Sarah released her left hand and placed it next to Lani's as if comparing skin colors. Then she pursed her lips as to say, "Yes, I'm two shades lighter than you are."

A shiver went through Lani's spine. *What's this all about? Who's the lightest, who's the darkest?* She'd never worried about that before, even though she'd noticed the two slaves working for Missus Tate in the big house were both very light-skinned. She half-smiled at Sarah, yanked the wet pants to herself, balled them up, and dropped them into the tub on the ground. Being the 'new girl,' she decided she'd tell this Sarah later that she's no more important, just because she's lighter skinned. Thank goodness her mother had worked with her on remaining calm. Still, she needed to let Sarah know and *all* the girls around this blazing fire, regardless of what shade of brown they were– they were sweating slaves and smelled like smoke.

To avoid talking, she reached into the cloudy, rinse water and pulled up a threadbare dress and waited. Sarah grabbed the other end, and they rang the water out. The late morning sun beamed and stung her tired back. How refreshing it would be if she could duck her head into the washtub for ten seconds.

The other girls seemed excited to finally hear Lani's voice, for she hadn't spoken much since being there only a week. They started making their way over around Sarah and Lani.

"Yes," Sarah continued, "you've got to watch the sparks around this fire, okay. See all these ash burns on my dress." She stood back and pointed to black holes all over her dress.

"Mine too. And it would be good if some boys helped us draw up and haul water," yelled another girl with a blue rag on her head. She was the shortest in the group and always talked loudly.

The other girls nodded in agreement and grunted, "uh huh." Then this girl came closer to Lani with a friendly grin and fat cheeks. She introduced herself as Rosalind and appeared to *be* about fifteen. Nobody knew their exact age. Her brown dress had burn spots too and was so thin— you could see her legs through it. Nicely, Lani gave Rosalind a closed-mouth hello smile and kept working. She noticed Sarah roll her eyes, as if to say Rosalind got on her nerves. Then the other girls came in closer, and Lani listened to them talk.

They chatted about getting ready for the fandanga, how they'd practiced the new song, and some boy that looked good last time. A flexible Rosalind stood back and did a high jumping movement, imitating how one of the adults danced, and all the girls burst out laughing.

Lani smiled politely and reached for the next shirt. She wanted to ask how and if any slaves had escaped from here. Before long, she did get up the nerve to ask them about a passage dance. To her disappointment, nobody remembered or had heard of that.

Out of the corner of her eye, she saw the patrolling overseer approaching them on his horse, and a hush flowed over the girls. Everyone scattered instantly like startled flies back to work. Lani tensed up, unsure if she should return to the wash or rinse tub. Ace rode through staring them down, then thankfully, he galloped off.

Sarah leaned close to her and stated in a hushed voice, "Okay, I wish I could write to find my papa we left back in Georgia. See Mas Tate's rich father, Big Mas Tate, helped both his sons get started in Texas. And my mom and I and about ten others were brought with him to this state, when I's about five . . . watch yourself. You don't want the tree treatment."

"Tree?"

"When Ace or Mas Tate get real mad at ya. They tie you to a tree, call in all the workers to watch and . . . beat you."

Lani's eyes bucked. "You lying."

Sarah moaned, and her eyes darted back over her shoulders. Then she squeezed her forehead as if blocking out some memory and immediately pointed to the next load. Lani picked up a basket and dropped more clothes into the cloudy water.

Her head felt tight. There was an uneasy quietness as everyone assumed their duties. Margie sloshed water all over her dress while bringing fresh water from the creek. Ashes lifted and floated through the air, and she wondered what would make the overseers mad. Back home, if she messed up her father's fishing catch, or let her mother's bread burn, she might get in big trouble. She sighed.

Here it could be anything.

Right now, feeling so tired, she thought she saw daylight stars floating above. She ran through her mind how she could sneak in a little rest.

CHAPTER TEN

The big oak tree branches swayed in the wind, and finally, the sun went behind the clouds for a few minutes. Whew, a little shade. She just wanted to sit down. Glancing at her palms, they were puffy and wrinkly like an elephant's skin. And her knuckles were sore from scrubbing all those hard-stained clothes on a rub board. Were they washing for the whole community? She'd never seen that many clothes in her life. What if she could get behind a tree, sit down, and rest for one minute?

Even though her back and arms were sore, she looked around and did not see Ace nearby. Quickly, she volunteered to carry the next load of clothes to the clothesline. When she got close to the clothesline, she tripped on a rock and fell, spilling some shirts on the ground. Swiftly, she started putting the clothes back into the basket. Then suddenly, on purpose, she fell again, sneaking in a rest on the ground. For a few moments, she closed her eyes and exhaled.

The sound of cows lowing out in the pasture echoed over her. Before she could get relaxed, however, she felt something sting her back. She cried out in pain, and her eyes flew open to swat an insect. It was not a bug.

Ace's whip came down on her back. Again. Lani rolled over, grabbed the clothes basket, and darted out of the way seconds before he lashed her a third time. She didn't dare look back while racing towards a giant oak tree.

Safely behind it, she stopped. Catching her breath and shaking, she peeked around the large tree trunk. Thankfully, Ace had already ridden off hollering at someone to "get a move on you." Before he got far, he suddenly pulled back on the reins of the tan horse and faced her. She slammed back against the tree, trembling. "You're due a whipping this week, gal," he shouted at her, then kicked the horse in the side, and galloped away into the cotton field.

She cautiously crept out after shaking for about five minutes. What did a whipping involve, and where? She felt a dense ball of dread in her stomach and viciously rocked back and forth. "Oh, I must find a way out of this disgusting place. I'm used to running through thickets, and long vines, but which direction . . ." she muttered, reaching for a wet cloth. The evening sun hung right above the tall trees on the west side of the plantation. Dabbing at her eyes, she picked up the basket and finished hanging out the clothes.

At bedtime in the cabin that night, Lani could only lay on her stomach. She was exhausted, scared, and her back stung and twanged. When Miss Martha came over to blow out the last lantern, she felt her hovering over her a minute. The motherly lady whispered and asked her about the bloodstains seeping through her dress, and if she was alright.

Lani mumbled, "I be better in the morning."

"Hold on, sweetie, I've got some grease for those cuts," she said, leaving with the light, as Lani's corner became dark.

How she wished Toluwani was here to comfort her. Rolling over to face the wall, she listened quietly as her cabin mates tried reassuring her while talking among themselves. She sensed Wil'm coming closer to her. His father had run away, and he loved asking questions.

"I done worse than that and got away with it," Wil'm said, scooting near her pallet. "You from Africa? Did they have lions in your backyard?"

Lani snickered. Then she turned back onto her hands, facing him. "Yea. Africa. Deep blue oceans, big mountains, and green forests. And no. No lions or tigers in our yard. If we did, little boys who had no shirts, like you, would be a good meal. Now, no talk to me." She crossed her arms and ducked her face down on the pallet.

"Ohh!" Wil'm hugged his chest, grabbed his quilt, and dove onto his pallet covering his head.

While Miss Martha treated her cuts, the girls in the cabin kept talking to her, and each other, about how ol' Ace would forget about that little matter of whipping her. Probably.

Lani heard the others snoring hours later, but even still, she tossed and turned. Completely frustrated, she realized real soon it'd be time to get up again for another wash day or help in the field from sunup in the beaming hot sun to sundown. Unbelievable. Perhaps she could find out who helped Wil'm's father run away. Where did he go? Did he go up north, or way south to Mexico? Then her heart fell two inches as she remembered the old map Lettie Mae had shown her that the slaves had found. The distance from Texas to a free country called Canada was even farther. "Oh, but I'm not afraid of running through thick woods, or swimming across a deep river," she whispered, closing her eyes.

On a Thursday morning a couple of days later, drunk with sleep, she staggered outside. Her body felt weighed down. After breakfast, she kicked at a chicken running across her path to the cotton field. Nothing made sense. The chicken squawked and fluttered in the air, hurrying away from her. She stopped and twisted her back. Even with the grease Miss Martha had applied to it, her back still throbbed in pain. A confused Lani watched the other chickens scamper to catch up with each other. It seemed the chickens had more freedom than her.

Making it to the field, she saw a few women wearing old ankle-length dresses down on their knees pulling at thick grass or weeds. Across from them were some men and older boys with tattered long-sleeved shirts chopping at the new cotton stalks. While they worked she heard them singing whinily, and holding-the-notes-too-long songs floating across the rows. Then she spotted Felix signaling her. He was the 'head man in charge' in the fields. When she got closer, she observed his coffee brown skin and gray speckles were sprinkled throughout his black wooly hair. The workers knew him as a—no-nonsense type of field boss.

Yes, she'd noticed how Mr. Tate came to Felix daily for his opinion on planting issues, what the sick mule needed, and general concerns that kept the plantation going. She'd even learned he'd taught Felix to count and figure amounts. Sometimes Felix would come up beside a worker and say his famous words, "we not gonna waste a good day's work 'specting a lousy crop."

"Come heah, Gal. Get this hoe," Felix said, with his ragged britches and big bare feet covered in dust. He threw the hoe toward her.

Lani picked up her pace and hurried to get the hoe since she wanted to be seen working when Ace made his rounds. Maybe he'd forget about her resting yesterday. Meanwhile, before she could pick up the hoe, she saw fear cross Felix's face like something awful was coming up behind her.

She jerked her head around just as a winded Ace trotted up next to her on his horse. He pulled back on the reins. The horse rocked back and forth, snorting like it expected the man to go on further.

"Hold on, Felix. That gal there needs a beating today. I'll have no lazy workers." Ace's sweaty hair clung to his forehead. He scowled at them both.

Lani was crippled in fear. Her legs twitched, and she began snickering uncontrollably. Felix stepped closer to her and stood by her side. She checked behind and in front of her and began feeling faint. It just so happened Mr. Tate had started making his rounds in the cotton fields. He rushed across the rows with long strides towards where his two trusted leaders were in a standoff.

Felix picked up her hoe and held it in his hand as her eyes darted from one man to the other. She saw confidence in Felix as he spread his legs wide. Then he turned to speak to Mr. Tate.

"Mas Tate, Suh. We need to show this gal, now, how to get this here grass out the way. Wez got a good crop started this year, Suh," he said, and he calmly turned and gazed up at Ace. It was not a 'I dare you' look, but more of a 'I know what the fields need' gaze even though he knew Ace could pop him with a whip at any moment.

Saying a soft prayer, she gritted her teeth to hold in more laughter. Her eyes started watering as she listened to Felix plead his case to Mr. Tate. Really, Felix was talking to Ace, too. Felix fanned his hand out over the abundant new crop.

Mr. Tate said nothing. He bent down to examine a new budding plant. The hoes hitting the ground were the only sound in the eerie silence as they waited for him to respond. It was only a couple of minutes, yet still, Lani believed her heart would pound a hole through her chest.

Before Tate straightened up, Ace signaled a worker to hold his horse. He refused to wait any longer. He knew how to handle new workers and hopped down with his whip.

Lani felt weak in her knees and crumpled to the ground. All the chopping and clicking sounds came to a sudden halt. She silently wept as she lay between two cotton rows. To keep her senses, she dug her fingernails into her arm and moaned. She just knew she would die. Ace ran over and grabbed her by the arm, and the scared girl screamed like an attacked tiger. Then he started dragging her like a sack past several workers who stood back helpless. She hoped they could save her, but abruptly they looked away.

Through her tears, she worried about the courageous Sarah who stepped out to follow them with panic, then anger, showing on her face. Immediately. Sarah stopped short when Ace raised his arm with the whip signaling everyone 'they'd better stay back.' Then he picked up his pace, pulling her towards the end of a row. Felix ran back to Mr. Tate and raised both hands for him to please stop the crazy man.

"Let her go," the plantation owner yelled loud and clear so all would know. He was the boss. Maybe he based his decision on which leader had the most experience. Ace two years. Felix over ten years.

Lani lay on the ground, almost heaving. She listened to see what Mr. Tate would say next and prayed, "*Onise Nla*, great God, please," she whispered.

"We got a meeting in town to attend today, Ace," Mr. Tate instructed and pulled a watch out of his pocket attached to a silver chain. At times like this, he considered going back to Georgia to help his father manage the corn and grain grist mills.

Ace stopped abruptly and frowned. He scowled first at Tate, and then at Felix. He barked a crazy laugh, backed up in a fury, and kicked dirt violently on Lani with his right foot with his face all twisted up.

"Here," Ace gestured to Felix. "Get over here and show her what to do. And there'd better not be one, chopped, cotton stalk," he said, popping his whip in the air. Then he nodded like I'll get you next time. Watching Tate, he threw his hands up and marched back to his horse.

Lani covered her face with her hands and rolled over on her back. She trembled from her scalp to her big toe. Blackbirds flew quietly overhead. Exhausted and weak, she pushed herself up. Then she started rubbing the dirt from her gritty arms. In all her days around here, she'd never seen the workers receive pity or rest. While she hiccupped and panted for breath, several girls rushed over helping her wipe dirt off her dress and wet cheeks.

Over to her left, Agibe renamed Ben, stood pounding his fist against his thighs, gazing at her with cold eyes. Remembering to hold her head up and avoid the stares, she headed toward Felix while wiping her nose. Within seconds, a lady burst out into a moaning song. One by one, the others joined in making a harmonious sound. Next, someone picked up the tempo and it became a more upbeat, hand-clapping type chant about the devils on earth, and swing low, sweet chariot: she wondered what a chariot could be.

"Whatever, if anything can carry me out of here, that'd be wonderful. That horrible Ace is a *buru,* evil man," she mumbled to herself while listening to the songs, and trudged closer to Felix. She planned next week to get up the nerve and ask about how many slaves had safely left Tate's work pens. Also, she would teach the girls a more upbeat song she knew from back home. Wonder where did the man who jumped and swam away from her second ship go? She lifted her hoe, chopped, and hacked angrily at the thick grass.

CHAPTER ELEVEN

On a Sunday evening late in July, Lani reluctantly peeked out her window. There was a drumbeat vibrating across the yard. *Bum bum, bum ba bum bum.*

The workers were gathered outside under the trees at the edge of the yard, singing and resting. Even a couple of new people were out there while their masters visited with the Tates. If she went back outside and stood around, maybe an elder would talk freedom talk.

Why on earth were unfree workers out singing and clapping? Surely, they knew Mr. Tate was just trying to keep them happy so they wouldn't run away.

She'd learned over the past weeks that several slaves had escaped and never been caught or brought back. That gave her hope, but they'd taken a big chance with their life. If she ran too, where would she stay? If caught, would she be brought back, or punished? She blocked the thoughts from her mind and watched one of the older ladies outside break out into a clapping fit on the right under the sweet gum tree.

Whoops! Sarah was coming back towards the cabins. Lani ducked down so she wouldn't see her inside.

"Lani, come on out, okay. You'll enjoy it," the 'boss girl,' as she'd secretly named Sarah, shouted through the open window. Her bubbly voice drifted over to her.

"No face masks. No practiced steps. Just standing around unda some trees. No thanks," Lani exclaimed. Then she leaned back against the wall, listening for Sarah to go away. That Sarah. Just because she was one year older and born in this country did not mean she knew everything. Lani adjusted the lumps in her so-called bed. Still she had to admit, Sarah was alright, for she always tried to include her in group activities, like jump rope or circle games.

She just felt completely out of place at the gathering. She did not recognize any of the songs. The girls would probably laugh at her ekun or tiger song, anyway. Oh, she so missed her family. My, my, she remembered running with Molayo through the thick sand back on the island. And if she'd been back home with all this music, her mother would've been all dressed up. Probably strutting in a dress she'd hand sewn with a matching green-with-wavy-white-lines headwrap. And she and her village friends tickled and chatting.

She did not want to be bothered today.

Bum, a bum rang outside now. Left knee, clap, twist—no, right. She tried hard to remember the beginning of the passage dance. Restless, she stretched her neck back out the window after fifteen minutes just to see better. Felix held something new this time, which created a high-pitched sound. A flat gourd-shaped thing rested under his chin, and he pulled a bow over the strings. A few small children ran back and forth, and a couple of older men sat on the ground staring out into the forest. She heard bursts of loud laughter from time to time.

Maybe she'd join Sarah and the group outside next week. Perhaps not. The music stopped, and she heard more voices of people returning to their shacks for the night.

"Soon," Lettie Mae said, entering the door, "you'll find out what you're made of around here come cotton-picking time. So, we 'preciate a break when we get one."

"How can it get worse? I already feel like a workhorse," she muttered to herself. Then she turned around and gazed at the heater in the middle of the room.

There were so many dumb things inside and outside, like that big heater taking up space in a cramped one-room cabin. It was one more thing reminding her of the heat. Although Margie kept saying, "Oh, we will need it this winter." She flopped back onto her pallet and massaged her fingers from her little finger to her thumb. Left knee up, clap, twist the hip, right knee up, clap.

The searing August heat dried up the grass, water holes, and flared folk's tempers, too. Warm summer nights and days had cracked open the now brown bolls which held the fluffy cotton. No one told her collecting Mr. Tate's cash crop, cotton, hurt.

On a Wednesday morning, Lani stood patiently listening. It was her first day of picking the soft white blooms. Felix showed her how to gently reach into the sharp needles holding the cotton and pull it out.

"Gets many in yo hands you can hold," he demonstrated with badly bent fingers. "Then ya drop them in this here tow sack," he said, gently tying a cotton sack around her right shoulder. The bottom swung down to her left waist. He stepped to the next stalk in a bent posture, which probably explained why his back stayed stooped when he walked.

Lani's hand quivered as she watched Sarah quietly pick cotton on the other row. Cautiously, she reached into the pointed needles and pulled out her first blossom. It felt like she was holding a piece of cloud. "It gonna take lots of these balls to fill up this sack," she said, dropping a handful into her sack. She grunted, feeling overwhelmed.

Felix sucked through his missing teeth. "Yep, as you can see, there's plenty," he did a hiccupping laugh, and marched across the next row, lifting Lettie Mae's full bag.

She pulled at her ear, wondering if that busy Mr. Felix had given up on leaving this plantation, or seen too much to risk it. Watching the busy workers, she noticed there was no casual talk. Just humming and picking. And the girls and ladies seemed to have fuller cotton sacks. Probably, she decided, because their fingers were slender and they could more easily get between the thick needles to snatch the cotton out.

If only she could tune up and start a tribal song. Instead, she hummed one to herself. *Ninu ewu,* survive, until free. Softly, then louder, she sang to move time along. At quitting time about five hours later, she had scratches all over her fingers and wrists. Glancing down, she became horrified at the sight of bloodstains all over her dress from where she'd been wiping her pricked fingers.

Some workers began mulling in washing up and stretching out, like seashells being washed ashore, all over the yard. Lani dropped down exhausted onto the sandy yard under an oak tree nearest the kitchen. Whew! She tried hard deciding after working all day, which smelled worse, musty mules or musty people. Soon, Miss Martha and her helper for the day would ring the supper bell. One after the other, Sarah, Lettie Mae, Margie, and Rosalind flopped down near her.

"I hope it's not peas again," Lani said, fanning herself with her dress tail.

"Youza get used to eating peas every day. Jes add the corn-bread," Lettie Mae suggested.

"Sho nuff?" Lani parroted.

Rosalind leaned over and whispered something to the agreeable Lettie Mae, and they glanced at Lani and both giggled.

Lani bristled. She was about tired of Rosalind making fun of her. Yes, she'd noticed different ones snickering behind her back about her accent. Just one more time and she would let

Rosalind have it. And that Lettie Mae. If it weren't that the skillful girl could take some pork lard and plait or twist up some pretty hairstyles on folks, she'd hit both of them.

"If we have a good cotton crop, okay, Missus Tate may tell Miss Martha to cook us some teacakes," Sarah added, rubbing her hands together and shifting the talk to food.

Lani drummed her fingers in the dirt and huffed. "I just wanna wade in the creek. And pretend it tez the ocean."

"Your words sound funny. Slow down when you talk. I can't understand what you done said," Rosalind blurted out. She dabbed at her sweaty armpits with scratches all over her fingers, expecting a laugh.

"Well, if you cleaned the slush out yo ears," Lani snapped, pointing to her ear.

Rosalind raised onto one knee coming at Lani.

Immediately, Sarah grabbed Rosalind's arm, stopping her. "Come on. It's about time to eat." She pulled Rosalind up, and Lettie Mae followed.

Sarah dragged a resisting Rosalind, who turned back around and pumped her shoulders at Lani. Instantly, Lani bucked back at her, rocked, and sprang up. Rosalind quickly hopped back. A strong Margie immediately rushed over and held Lani back.

Lani puffed and shook her head, then she said to Margie, "She talking about me. And I'm still trying to know what she's saying most of the time. Like, sho nuff, I reckon, direckly . . . please." She squeezed her dress to calm down. Out of nowhere, her stomach growled loudly, and they both giggled.

Sitting back down, she thanked Margie for holding her back. Then she drew figures in the dirt as they waited. Margie took her head rag off and fanned herself. Since Margie was tall with a long neck and long legs, Lani figured she'd be an easy sew for a custom dressmaker. And she always tried to keep the peace. The line formed in front of them as more workers picked up their tin plates.

"Well, you may not know it, but Rosalind's father got beat so bad for running off. His cuts became infected. Then Mas Tate soon sold 'em and fired the other overseer we had," Margie said, breaking the silence.

Lani looked at her grimly. "Humph. We could all compare unthinkable memories. My mother and I made it as a pair from Africa to the island. Then they sent my moeder away... Still, it no give Rosalind the right to keep picking on me." Lani swallowed hard.

"I know . . . but guess what Sarah told me?" Margie continued. "The fellow that keeps helping you carry your field rakes? Remember? The one who keeps flexing his muscles in front of you? He'd told her with your lovely round face, and sweet brown eyes, yousa the pretties' gal he'd seen," she offered, giving Lani a quick pinch.

"Well . . . uh . . . I reckon," Lani said, squeezing her lips tightly, holding in a smile.

Of course, she remembered the warm feeling spreading all over her when she was near Ben. They hadn't talked on the third boat ride. But he'd tried more than once over the past months to speak with her. However, he seemed always to get tongue-tied. She glanced secretly over at him now standing with a group of men. His broad shoulders showed through his raggedy, short-sleeved shirt. And every time she turned around, he always smiled at her a bit too long. Still, she felt confused about the new giddy feeling she got when he looked at her.

Rubbing her grumbling stomach, she asked Margie, "Do you believe what the house slave said last Thursday, about a Harriet lady?"

"What? Yea, I believe it. Said the rumor is, a Harriet Tubman helped slaves to escape to freedom up north," Margie said, smacking her lips like it was a fact.

Lani felt her first leap of hope in her throat that freedom was possible. Then the supper bell's tingling rang across the yard. She got up smiling. Nobody had to be called twice.

Today, like most days, she dabbed the peas and hot corn-bread with her fingers and gobbled them down. Over to her left, she scanned the rows of remaining white cotton balls. "After all that cotton's picked, I'm sure going to get dressed up, and stay, at the next fandanga," she mumbled. How she wished a wind storm would come through and blow all that cotton miles away.

Her droopy eyelids pushed down. Completely worn-out, she fell over asleep with her supper plate still in her hand.

CHAPTER TWELVE

On a Sunday evening in October, Lani stood outside her cabin door determined to join the group of young people standing under a different tree away from the adults. A crisp fall breeze blew golden and crimson red oak leaves all over the yard. The Tates had stopped all the dancing and carrying on during the cotton-picking season. People were too tired by Sunday, anyway.

So, after six weeks of back-breaking labor, by October, a weary Lani gladly got ready for a gathering. She patted her hair, hoping it looked alright. Strolling up the lane, she ran her hand down her faded blue dress. "Well," she grunted, "this is the best dress I could find in that pile of clothes." Pulling her shoulders back, she elevated her head and eased towards the edge of the group.

The yard dogs barked sporadically at the crowd's noises to the left of the cabins. They always seem irritated by all the banging, whistling, clapping and carrying on under the trees.

She called a collie dog over and patted his head to calm him, and herself, down. Then the dog rolled over for her to rub its belly. She felt quite proud of herself for learning how to quieten the dogs.

Scratching her forefinger helped her relax as she strolled closer to the gathering. She spotted Sarah with her hair greased down and pulled back into a bun. More conscious of how her hair might look, Lani patted the frizzy parts which had separated from her plaits. "Hope I don't look a hot mess," she mumbled to herself. Last night she'd washed, oiled, and parted her hair into small sections. Then pulled real hard to create short plaits or braids and interlocked them together.

Luckily, she noticed Margie with a top plait already coming a loose, and part of her hair sticking straight up like an unraveling rope. The yapping Rosalind stopped talking and turned towards Lani, looking her up and down. This made Lani want to turn around and go back inside the cabin. No. Even though Rosalind had her mouth all twisted up, she ignored her because Rosalind looked no better. She had pieces of bed covers tied to the ends of her six plaits in two different colors, off-white and brown. And also, a lot of the young ladies' foreheads, arms, and legs were shining with lard or cow tally-fat. So, Lani felt she'd fit right in. Then Sarah signaled her over, and she did a quick-step of relief and joined the group.

Some adults standing under the other tree caused her to do a double take. With their faces now cleaned of dirt and grime, she struggled to recognize them.

"Who are they?" she asked Sarah, confused. Now that everyone had finally cleaned themselves up, there were more bright-skinned people here than she'd realized.

"That's Addie. She's just a 'wobbling and twisting her feet trying to stand straight in those tight winter shoes," Sarah added, grunting.

Lani smiled, then checked her own feet. She sure wished she had shoes to cover her crusty toes. But with Addie's face scrunched up like her feet hurt, Lani chuckled and thought being barefoot was much better.

A group of boys and young men were standing under the other oak tree. And she noticed Jeb, who was about eighteen, running out from the group squawking with laughter. He ran over and started hitting a plow and then ran back to the group, still laughing. She grinned. What could be so funny?

When she got closer to the musicians sitting out in a clearing between the two big trees, she took notice. One man blew into what looked like a cut off fishing pole with holes in it. Standing next to him was Mr. Felix, a'rocking and bobbing in rhythm while playing that fiddle. The drummer sat, all serious-faced, playing the drum made from cowhide pulled over a hollowed-out tree stump.

She inhaled deeply as the sweet smell of honeysuckle, rosemary, and cinnamon floated around them. It seemed like a lot of the ladies had soaked plants in water to make their special scented water. It smelled like a cooking kitchen out there. She leaned from side to side and turned around, hoping that someone would put on a little white clay face paint. Or she wished, at least, a group of people would line up and dance in unison. Nope. However, in a few minutes she felt lighter. Her head bobbed on its own to the wangling-type music, and she laughed at the showoffs doing some strange dance moves.

"Felix ez playing and dancing like he jumping over hot rocks," she uttered to Margie, standing next to her. The other girls nearby burst out laughing, and Sarah bent over in laughter. Lani felt, maybe finally, she was becoming part of the group. She covered her mouth, just a 'grinning. Too soon, the evening sun began setting, and the music stopped. Lani crossed her arms. "It's just not the same as back home," she grumbled to those near her who chattered and moved around.

No one answered her. Even Lettie Mae beside her, pulling at a dress which fit her a bit too tight, ignored Lani, also. Next, Rosalind started twisting and walking herself over to a group of boys, smiling a bit too hard. Lani shook her head at Rosalind.

For Lani, after so many Sunday evenings of staring at the walls wondering where Molayo and her mother were. Roaming around the creek checking for trails away from the plantation. Or making dirt houses with her feet, all of these pastimes were alright. But she soon found out how fast Mondays came. So standing there now she realized how much she enjoyed, and had missed, sharing in the company of other people on their only slightly free day of the week. She was glad she'd joined the group today.

Like most Sundays, Mr. and Mrs. Tate came out the back door of the big house to linger and listen to their talk. Most of the slaves lowered their voices or changed the subject until they went back inside.

Minutes later, when she gazed across at the boys, Ben's eyes were focused on her as he headed her way. Again, like before, she turned away from him and headed back to the cabin. As the wind shifted, a whiff of a rank sour smell from the hog pens covered the yard. Next month, folks said she'd have to help at the hog-killing time. That sounded too much.

As she entered her cabin, Felix was saying goodnight to Miss Martha near the door. She moved her pallet around and listened.

"I'm telling you, Martha, folks being snappier lately. The plantation owners are coming around more talking to Massa about an upcoming president 'lection. Which states for, or against slavery."

"Aye, Felix, we got to rest these tired bones. Give me a hug. And get to your cabin before dark." Miss Martha giggled. "G'won, I ain't studying 'bout you." Then she dipped her head inside the cabin, grinning.

Lani got tickled about that couple, lit the evening lamp, and wondered which states allowed people freedom. How close were those states to Texas? She held down a nervous laughter creeping up her throat from thinking about it. How would she get there? She started humming.

Soon it was November and most of the trees showed their skeletons with all their leaves gone, except for the pine trees. This allowed Lani a much broader view through the forest behind the plantation. Winter was coming. The pesky bugs and wild animals had gone or were busy preparing for the cold winter, and the people were working just as hard.

Why she'd never seen such boiling of jars, canning of corn, beans, tomatoes, cabbage chowchow, or any extra fruit and vegetables grown in the fields. Even the hulls. Slaves were busy hand rolling the kernels off dried corn, stomping dried peas, holding them up, letting the wind blow away the dried shells, or boiling sugarcane juice for syrup. A full-time restock of the storehouses and corn cribs happened—every day. Thankfully, the air outside felt cooler.

After breakfast on a Tuesday, a piercing, squealing and squalling sound suddenly startled her. She strained to see what it could be while hurrying towards the fields. It was the grayish-black hogs lined up for slaughter down near the hog pen. She stuck a finger in her ear and wanted to cover her eyes and not look at the squalling pigs. It reminded her of the screaming and fighting when her village was captured. Her insides trembled.

Then a galloping Ace caught up with her. "Hey, go help with the cracklings." He pointed up front.

She skipped and walked faster. Oh, she could hardly function when he patrolled anywhere near her. She almost wet herself. He always rode around on his horse, jerking his head here, stopping, and staring at folks. She hoped he'd get a crook in his neck.

For she'd seen him pull a grown man out and whip him, just for going to get water before water break.

To her right, Ben and Jeb were pulling and pushing a long saw with handles on each end through a big log. Back and forth they went, push, pull, lean forward, lean backward, as sawdust flew everywhere. Other men were stacking firewood and splitting logs with an ax — one swing at a time.

"No wonder Ben has those big muscular arms. When he finally gets away from here and becomes a free man, I just know he'll do good as a paid house builder," she muttered, then strolled hastily by the men while throwing smiles towards Ben.

Uh-oh. Impatiently, Ace yelled louder in her direction as his hands jabbed hard at her to join an older lady and Sarah working around the black pot. Now. She wondered how he kept up with *everyone*.

At least she did not have to help iron all Mr. Tate's shirts today. Because that would've meant heating and lifting a heavy metal iron onto a hot stovetop. Mixing the powder starch and sprinkling it on the clothes. Then jumping back from the burning steam and hoping not to scorch a brown hole in the clothes, or your fingers.

A fire blazed wildly under the pot where Sarah stood. She stopped.

"Okay, we gone cook the pig skins in here. Watch for popping grease," Sarah told her while yawning.

Lani grimaced, puzzled. At the edge of the yard, Margie and Lettie Mae were dipping and pulling something up out of a tub.

"My that looks like cooler work," she said, pointing at Lettie Mae.

Sarah kept stirring the cooking cracklings, and Lani inhaled the wonderful smoky smell of the frying meat.

"Well, just be glad you didn't get stuck cleaning chitlins or guts today," Sarah said, squishing her reddening face. "We get to eat what Massa don't want on the hog. And I hate cleaning them, but they make a good meal."

Lani smirked like she had a bad taste in her mouth. "Sometimes, I wonder what the cooks put in the pots around here. But when you're hungry. . ." She hopped back as hot grease popped in the air.

They both chuckled, and Sarah added more skins to the iron kettle. Lani thought about the hogs. They waddled near the creek bottom, and a creek leads to a river, and she knew first hand that the river ran into the big ocean. She added sticks to the fire, then whispered to Sarah, "Last night, I heard crunching and voices behind the cabin, and peeked outside. I saw pine tar lights, and it was several of the slave men darting back from the thickets."

"Who?" Sarah looked around cautiously. "Some men are planning an escape and they meet in the woods at night."

"When? Can we join 'em?" Lani asked, knowing she could tell them the route back to town.

"Only if they ask you, now back to work."

Lani grunted, then poked at the fire while thinking of who would go with her.

It was a Friday about mid-morning in late December, and they'd been stuck inside for two days. The freezing wind whistled through the cracks of their cabin's thin walls. For sure, Margie was right. They needed that heater.

Miss Martha told Lani it was her turn to go outside and bring in wood. She piled on two old coats and grumbled. Opening the door, cold air stung her face. She ducked and ran like someone was chasing her to the woodpile. After stacking several sticks of wood in her arms, she raced back inside.

"Ahh, my feet, ears, nose, burn." She wiggled her cold fingers and dumped the wood in the corner while shivering. Her cabin mates huddled around the heater nodding their heads.

Then Lani backed up to the roaring fire in the wood heater warming her backside, but her ears still felt frozen. As soon as she turned around to warm her hands, her back became cold again. She slowly took her feet out of her second-hand men's shoes that the girls received for the winter, pulled off her threadbare socks, and massaged her cold toes.

Her first winter.

She soon realized a person *could* wear three pairs of pants if it meant staying warm. Yes, the workers got one change of clothes, and bare necessities to remain alive. Still, thin coats and threadbare quilts were not much protection in airy shacks or outside.

After shaking her hurting hands forcefully until she got circulation back in them, they made string figures with old thread. Then they drew pictures in the dirt floor or sang songs—anything to pass the time. She daydreamt of the different cloth designs she could make which would give her strength, or meaning. It'd be nice if she could sell the cloth.

Before she went to sleep in her corner that night, she warmed her patched quilt against the heater, then ran and jumped under it onto the pallet with her teeth chattering. Sometime in the middle of the night, she woke up feeling immobilized. For a thoughtful Miss Martha had gone around and dropped another clothes-stuffed quilt on her and the others. With all those quilts on her, she could barely move. Even so, she slept warmer.

The next morning, Sam'l started screaming, "It's snowing!" waking everybody up.

"What, where?" Lani eased out from under her covers and gazed outside, and immediately her eyes widened. Her heart leaped at the sight of what looked like pieces of white cotton floating peacefully down and covering the otherwise messy yard.

East, west, the chairs under the trees, the wagons, and even the shacks' rooftops were covered entirely in white. Cold or not, she had to get outside and touch it.

Her cabin mates yelled at her to "close the door." Giddy, she hurriedly put on her big shoes and stepped outside. Looking behind her after lifting her feet, she saw her shoe prints trailing her. Wow, white snow covered the drooping pine tree needles, the fence posts, and the endless empty fields behind them. Tickled, she reached down and picked up the wet powder, and it melted in her hands. Then she leaned her head all the way back to catch the falling snow in her mouth.

"Get back in here before you freeze," Margie blurted outside and slammed the door.

Lani felt wet and cold and tingly when she zipped back inside. Shedding her wet freezing clothes, she wrapped up in a quilt. How she wished her cousins and brothers back home could see this. It seemed like God had sent a glistening winter gift falling peacefully outside, giving them a day of rest.

January was around the corner, and Mr. Tate and his neighbors were having a New Year's Eve party next Saturday, if the muddy roads were passable. As soon as the snow melted, there'd be work to do. The slaves had to gather wood, draw up water, and trudge through the cold winds to tend and feed the animals while the Tates warmed themselves by their fireplace inside.

Lani flopped into a wobbly chair thinking how next year she'd be older, and she'd already noticed more developing changes about her body. New hair sprouted from her head to her legs. For now, she savored being able to rest and admire the new white blanket covering the yard. Temporarily, she prevented 'why' questions from entering her mind.

CHAPTER THIRTEEN

L ani wondered why her stomach hurt so. She woke up and cringed a second time. Maybe she'd eaten too many wild juicy blackberries yesterday.

It was still dark outside her window, so she dreaded going to the outhouse alone. It hit again, causing her to double over in pain. This cramp was a different type. It felt like a knife being pulled across the lower part of her stomach. If not having 'a say so' of what you did every day, what you ate, when, and if, you could rest wasn't enough— to be sick and still have to work was torture.

Texas had become one hot, dry, and dusty state by this Friday morning in late May 1860. Very little rain had fallen during the springtime. She'd worked for free for one whole year. White folks came talking about the fear of fires breaking out. Surprisingly, Mr. Tate hired out Jeb to dig the neighbors' water wells deeper, and allowed him to get paid something. What type of work could she do and possibly get paid, too?

"Ouch," she moaned. She wanted to spare her cabin mates the misery of hearing a bunch of pooting noises, along with stinky smells. So, she passed on using the chamber pot at the back of the room. Fumbling for a coal oil lamp, she lit it and trotted outside.

Another hard cramp hit, so she stopped, grabbed her stomach, about ready to call someone. Oh, how she missed her mother and aunties for advice. Once inside the outhouse, she checked herself and found she was passing blood. "Oh my, this is what the girls talked about and were constantly asking each other, 'have you started yet?'" Her mind swirled. She massaged her forehead. What to do next? It was too early to wake up a tired sleeper.

Usually, some ladies had several rags they'd use and wash out as needed during their time of the month. While others just bled through their clothes as a daily occurrence. She'd observed this, and no one seemed shocked. This change happening to her now was so unexpected, though.

Did this mean she was now a real woman? In some ways, yes. "How can this be when no one's told me I'm ready for my rite of passage ceremony?" Straining to see the trail in the dark while walking back inside, she wondered if she was supposed to act differently. She halted, placed her hands on her much broader hips, and noticed how her chest now filled out her dresses more.

Then she eased quietly back into the cabin. After finding a rag, she flopped on the bed, and could hardly wait until daylight. Soon she'd tell Sarah and the other girls of this unexpected discovery. However, right after breakfast, before she could even stop and talk to the girls, Ace came a' bossing. Her orders were first to help gather eggs from the henhouse and then go straight to the gals under the tree making quilts.

What started as a cloudy morning soon cleared up, and the blue sky came through with white clouds showing different shapes and drawings above. She moped around the dried grass as it crunched under her feet and headed inside the henhouse.

"Yow." A hen pecked her hard for trying to steal the eggs from underneath her. Lani rubbed her throbbing knuckles. "Maybe I can show Missus Tate how I can make necklaces or something. Then get a pass. She takes me to town with her for supplies. I may meet other captives or someone to ask if they've seen my mother. They may know of a group of captives that came over from Africa about April of last year," she muttered, then hurried over to the ladies out under the big oak tree.

The three ladies were rolling a quilt out between two wooden horses. Oh, the idea of taking plain cloth and cutting and shaping it into something different, excited her. Plus, it was in-the-shade work. When she reached the quilters, she eyed a cloth scrap box filled with stacks of empty cotton flour sacks that had lovely blue and yellow flowers on them. Besides that were bolts of cloth in solid black, purple, soft gold, and red. Two older ladies were bent over the quilt sewing thread trails from one side to the other. One lady had deep wrinkles all over her face while the other one kinda tilted her head to focus with a lazy eye. They mumbled among themselves as she approached.

Handing Lani a pair of scissors, Miss Martha showed her how to cut squares, triangles, or rectangular strips of material and lay them out to form a perfect square or block. Then she told her they would sew the blocks together next time. Miss Martha rejoined the other ladies.

After a while, Lani asked the busy ladies to check the first block she'd laid out on a chair. Miss Martha ambled over and examined how Lani had arranged the pieces together. She gazed at Lani puzzled, leaned her head left and right, checking behind Lani, and asked, "Where you get that?"

"I made it."

"Now listen. One thang I won't have is lying, cheating, or stealing," Miss Martha said, moving in closer to Lani's face. "Did you get the block from the big house?"

Lani blinked hard. "Um, no ma'am. I just put it together for you to approve," she said as her voice got higher.

Miss Martha stuck her needle into her apron and called the other ladies over to see the square that Lani had overlaid pieces of fabric together. It had solid purple rectangle strips on the top, bottom, and sides, and four soft gold triangles inside the square on the top and bottom with four long red pieces making a cross in the middle.

The older lady with the wrinkles put her hands on her hips and grunted. She said, "That beat all I ever seen. Just pretty."

"Kut gracious allow," the one with the lazy eye leaned down close, then jumped back in amazement.

Lani stepped back, squeezing her sides. What had she done wrong? Her mind had already planned the layout for another square. After a couple of seconds, she relaxed when they told her to continue cutting.

When the ladies went back to stitching, she slipped several small strips of material into her pocket. Oh, she had plans. If she could get enough scraps, she'd make a block with a fish escaping its net then nail the cloth square on the otherwise drab, gray unpainted walls in their shack. It'd be a symbol of 'hope' for her and the cabin mates.

About midnight, when Lani had fallen into a deep sleep she got yanked off the pallet into the dirt.

"Move, Lani," an angry Miss Martha said, standing over her. She reached under her bed, searching for something. "I told you, if you steal you gonna get caught. Same for cheating and lying."

Lani's arms scrambled in the dirt. She was half asleep and trying to figure out where she was resting. She wondered if the voice was part of a nightmare.

"So, what's this you hiding under yo' bed?" Miss Martha demanded, holding up a ball of material scraps.

"I, me, I . . . only wanted to make more blocks," she croaked.

"What you will do, is take this material back to Missus Giruth's tomorrow." A frustrated Miss Martha pointed her finger at Lani. "Or I will beat yo' bonka, myself." Her thin cotton nightdress made a trail in the dirt as she went back to her bed and blew out the lamp.

Shaking and wiping her nose, Lani sat up and sniffed. Ugh! The fact the whole house had witnessed her shame upset and embarrassed her. Her face felt hot.

Soon the others stirred and moved around in their beds, probably trying to go back to sleep. How could she be hollered at outside, and inside the cabin too? *Can't keep anything for yourself? Not even scraps?* Oh, she hated this whole place. Who knew what Missus Tate would do to her for punishment.

Once the first rooster crowed early the next morning, Lani rolled anxiously out of bed, picked up the odds and ends of cloth and thread, then she tip-toed across the yard to the quilting box. Thankfully, it had been covered and remained under the trees. A dog barked at her, and she signaled it over to her and patted his head to calm him down. Hopefully, she would get this done before someone came outside. The running had made her palms sweaty. After she replaced the material, she prayed Missus Tate and Miss Martha would please forget about it. Heading back, she planned to apologize to Miss Martha for disappointing her. She slipped back inside to her pallet.

Fortunately, in the afternoon there were already major problems in the big house so she escaped a public beating, this time. The Tate family were having a big family meeting. Word was Missus Giruth was crying hysterically over the possibility both their sons could be called to fight if there were indeed a Civil War. When the news about the Tates' sons reached the field, Lani wondered what a civil war was.

"If this war is like two tribal wars back home, I sure hope I don't have to hide again." She looked out over the withering cotton stalks in desperate need of rain and chopped at the dried weeds. To make up for her trouble, she decided to offer to pick more wild blackberries for Miss Martha to make a sticky, sweet blackberry cobbler.

That would also give her another chance to look at how she might follow a deer or animal trail through the woods, which ran close to the roadway.

CHAPTER FOURTEEN

Rosalind, Lani, and Sarah picked up their baskets an entire year later in April 1861, on a Saturday evening. They set out to find poke salad or wild greens for supper. Tonight, Lani hoped she could fall asleep without hunger pains stabbing her under the ribs again. After lifting her long dress caught on a thorny vine, she hurried across the thicket.

How had she made it through another year of hard work? She sighed, realizing things were bad for the masters this year when the workers had to scavenge the woods for something extra to eat. This country had gone through lots of changes. And, yes, the Civil War had begun.

"There's gotta be some warriors fighting hard to free us slaves," she said to herself, rushing to keep up with Rosalind's quick steps. Yesterday someone had said there were two presidents over this divided country now. A Jefferson Davis was the Confederate States president, which included Texas. And Abraham Lincoln was the Union president. Lani wondered how and if that'd make a difference to her in being freed.

Spring, with its new life of fresh grass, green leaves, and wildflowers symbolized new starts and offered new hope. Yes, two more slaves had escaped, and no, they did not take Lani with them. But she remained hopeful, listening for how she could escape, and when. Also, she'd become a regular with helping to sew things. If they only knew of the cloth drawings and quilt layout visions in her head. Jamesa gave them word on how people used quilts to recognize a safe house when running away. She had to learn those layouts. Or one day sell her dyed cloth.

Please, when the time was right, she wanted to run away too.

Both of Mr. Tate's sons were enlisted and away fighting in the war. The trips to the town's cotton gin were fewer and fewer. His cotton sales were down. And people were coming to the farm worried about changes to the way things were. Now when Mr. Tate's money was low, it meant near starvation for the workers. Something besides pot licker or vegetable broth and bread for supper would be helpful.

The lush green grass and tall weeds covered the ground as they searched for a trail in front of the house. At least with this duty, they'd sweat less, and get to see the different golden, purple, and orange wildflowers among the trees.

"We gone have to cross the creek to get enough," Sarah directed with anticipation, pushing back vines and limbs.

"The cooks check before fixing anything to make sure it's not poison," Rosalind chimed in, smoothing her thick eyebrows down.

The woods were quiet except for the occasional *chia, chia, chia* from birds calling each other. Finding a shallow area in the creek east of the front yard, they waded across.

"There's some," Rosalind yelled and bent down, snapping the red-lined green leaves.

"Oh ye, we can use this plant to dye our clothes red," Lani said, with her mind turning about cloth patterns. Immediately, she missed her mother and wondered if her mother had enough to eat on the plantation where she lived. Back home she'd always say to her and her brothers, "eat all your food."

Stepping out closer to a new patch, Lani heard a thundering noise coming down the road. "Hush. I hear someone coming." She peered through the brush and trees ahead.

The girls all stood up, checking which direction to take if it was someone out chasing runaways. They didn't have a pass, and they were half a mile from home.

"Quick, let's hurry back across the creek, and we can hide behind a bush before they cross the bridge up there," Lani suggested and started moving towards the bridge. Her curiosity of seeing new people and what the riders may be talking about, got to her.

"You crazy?" Sarah said with shock. "We cannot swim. We're heading home, right now."

Rosalind stood, hesitated, then swiftly grabbed her basket, and followed a fast Sarah rushing back through the thicket and trees. Lani decided to take a chance so she sprinted farther out to the bridge. She waded into the murky water without a splash and watched the other two girls trot back towards the front yard. Then she swam to a deeper part of the creek, past the bridge, and hid behind a fallen tree trunk on the ledge of the riverbank.

The horses' hooves clopping became louder. She could see four men with cowboy hats riding along and arguing loudly. She understood a few words and phrases like, "Tate's got to pay," "he needs a beat down," and "we've got a war going on, and all along he keeps saying there's got to be a better way. Traitor."

One man with a long hooked nose roared, "Tate's tried every rule possible to keep his boys out the war. Now, if his father didn't own those large grist mills in Georgia, he'd stop all that. Yeah, told me his mother hated slavery and mistreatment of people. And, she tried to get a club going in Georgia to change the laws for slaves and women's rights."

"What?" The older looking one yelled, and yanked back on his horse. " A bunch of mess! We tore up Mr. Joe's house and barn last week for no-war-crazy talk. And Johnny here seen Tate uptown an hour ago. So today, is the day."

"And if we see any stray runaways, it'd be a good day to catch one," the younger one with a red bandana around his neck added.

The horses trotted across the bridge, and Lani's chest started beating so fast it caused her to shake the tree limb she clenched. If the men checked the water, they would see the frightened girl hovering behind the shaking tree. No doubt she'd be beaten, or worse.

Within minutes, the men had passed. She slowed her breathing, waiting for what seemed like forever in case they turned around. Checking the water for snakes or curious turtles floating near her, she quietly creeped out of the water dripping wet. She had to hurry back and warn somebody. Left or right? Should she take a chance on going straight to the big house without permission: the front door and all? That was absolutely forbidden. Ace had gone for the day. Mr. Tate wasn't back yet. Plus, Felix wouldn't believe her.

She dropped her basket and dashed through the tall grass. What if they burned the *buburu*—evil, heartless, awful—plantation down? She'd wished it'd happened many times. Then surely, she'd get away from here. Nothing belonged to her, not even herself. All of it was Mr. Tate's property. No one would listen to her. Let the whole farm burn.

Or run? This is it, my chance to run away. After entering the edge of the yard, breathless, she stopped. Abruptly her mother's voice came to her: *"This is your village. For now,"* this is where she lived.

Swiftly, she picked up her pace, raced up the steps across the front porch, and started banging on the front door. Her stomach tightened, filled with fear and adrenaline, which spurred her on. Jamesa, Missus Tate's house servant, answered the door with a face of shock then anger. Both of them could be tied with a rope and whipped for disobeying plantation rules.

"Eh ... Eh ... I got to tell Missus Tate there men in de woods," she stuttered, pointing back behind her and panting and coughing. Water puddled on the porch below her dress.

"Listen, child. I don't have time for foolishness. Now get away from here," Jamesa shouted, stepping out onto the porch with her clean white apron and matching white head rag on.

When someone knocked, Jamesa had to prepare her face. She was sweet for houseguests, submissive for the Tates, or ignore the unspoken envy from the workers upset that she dressed nicely and worked inside. However, Jamesa was the source of all knowledge about local, state, or national news. She heard everything by listening to Mas Tate and his visitors, who talked over her like her ears did not work.

Coming out right behind Jamesa, Missus Tate pushed her servant aside and stepped out with a frown about what, and who, could be banging on the front door.

"Missus, they're men saying they gonna burn this here place down," Lani forced out loudly around Jamesa who tried blocking her from speaking to the Missus. Lani's legs started shaking. For if she were lying, she'd be in big trouble. Her wet dress felt tight, and she anxiously pulled at it.

Scanning out east and west of the yard, Missus Tate fanned Lani away. "Get to the fields and help check for worms. One leaf at a time." Her silky hair was pulled up into a knot, and some loose strands draped her face. She studied Lani's boldness with steady blue eyes.

"Yes' um," Lani turned and headed down the steps feeling confused. If she'd only kept her mouth closed. She started angrily rubbing her wrists. She'd probably be made an example of and punished in front of the others.

That's when they heard a piercing scream from the back of the house. Uh-oh. Missus Tate and Jamesa ran back inside. Lani felt like someone had hit her in the stomach and bolted for the backyard. Others were running too. Some workers ran from the fields and some from their cabins. Chickens cackled, and the dogs ran wild, barking. The four cowboys had circled the plantation and come in through the backwoods.

One of them with his shirttail flying raced around breaking tools. Another one's straw hat fell off while he started throwing boards into a pile. Children, people, and animals were all frantic. Lani stopped and clutched her chest. Right there, the one with the long hook nose had grabbed Sarah. He had a silly grin on his face and yelled, "I got myself a pretty one here." Sarah howled and pulled back. Lani picked up a rock and hurled it at the man dragging Sarah by the arm. He hollered in pain, hopped on one foot, and released Sarah.

Meantime, the one without the hat behind her started knocking down the chicken pen, shattering boards. Lani turned, tripped, and fell in the dirt. When she stumbled up, her wet dress was covered in sticky mud, and she wiped icky chicken poop off her hands. Then another painful scream rang out. Miss Martha stood yelling in front of the smokehouse door closer to the front yard. Lani had to rescue her.

Before the other workers got there, the older man of the cowboys came outside the smokehouse throwing meat out on the ground. He turned and slapped the panicking woman across the face. Blood trickled from her nose. A rushing Felix hobbled in from the field behind them, holding his hoe way up ready to hack somebody. Lani raced on tip-toes right behind Felix.

Suddenly, a gunshot rang through the air. She dropped flat on the ground, like a dead woman. The dogs tucked their tails beneath them and raced for cover under the shed. The alarmed cowboys all ran for the closest shelter. With one eye, Lani saw a bold Missus Tate standing on the back porch with her gun preparing to fire again, but with so much movement she probably didn't know where to aim.

The one without the hat gawked back out from behind the outhouse looking frozen in shock. The scruffy man seemed stunned that a woman was standing there ready to shoot the next person that moved. Why he should have known that Tate would think all people had potential. Ladies could be a doctor, a lawyer, and even learn to use a weapon. What was wrong with him?

"We're leaving," the long-nosed one pleaded, dropping a board and hurrying behind the wagon shed. "Don't shoot." He stuck his hands way out.

"You got one minute to get off my land, or else," Missus Tate shrieked from the porch with one eye closed and her shooting eye ready.

The older man eased out and signaled the others to come out of hiding. They shuffled backward quickly to their horses, fumbling, yanking, and untying the restless stallions. Then only halfway in their saddles, they spurred and slapped the horses to get away quick.

Lani hopped up and guided Wil'm and several other young children behind the big house for safety. They huddled close to her, trembling. She knew they were afraid. She had to be brave for the children. She reminded herself of her mother's words, "somehow we will live on."

"It's almost over," she consoled Sam'l, who was looking up at her with a snaggletooth weak grin.

Then they heard "hi, hi" and a thundering of horses' hoofs galloping away. Calming herself and Sam'l, she then patted a shirtless Wil'm's back. The other children were almost standing on her toes, silently crying, and she hugged them, too. After a few minutes, a braver Lani pried herself away and peeked around the corner. The chickens were still running wild, and the now confident dogs were chasing the riders away, barking loudly. Missus Tate reached out for a porch post and fell back against it, just a shaking her head back and forth. Slowly, stiffly, she stumbled back inside.

Felix and Ben rushed over to help Miss Martha wobbling up off the ground. "Mas Tate be home soon," Felix directed everyone to get back to their work.

Lani gingerly strolled over towards the others who were all talking fast in disbelief about what had just happened. Her mouth felt dry, and she pressed her chest to calm down. Then she helped stack the broken boards into a pile. This Civil War about people's rights suddenly became more severe than anyone had imagined.

"Unreal. I haven't been able to escape, but I'm going to figure something out," she muttered, picking up a splintered chair and chucking it as hard as possible towards a tree.

Shortly later, standing at the well, she drew up fresh water to drink and clean her legs. Thankfully, the spring days were longer and they had more time outside. No one would be able to sleep much that night, anyway. The well boards squeaked as she pulled the thick rope attached to the heavy water bucket that inched its way up. Over to her right, Rosalind, Lettie Mae, and Margie assisted Sarah to the well. Sarah's eyes were puffy and red, and she still trembled. Lettie Mae dipped water into a pan and began wiping Sarah's arm, who sniffed quietly and held her head down.

Lani scooted in closer, sharing her drying rag with them. "Those nasty, smelly men. I'm glad they gone. We just like brown specks on a big white sandy beach. It takes all kinds to circle the ocean and make for a good foot massage."

"What you talking 'bout?" Rosalind snapped. "Every time we turn around, you talking about beaches, sand. All I know is we always got to rake Mas Tate's front yard, which is nothing but dirt."

"Oooh," Margie and Lettie Mae hooted, covering their mouths and laughing loudly.

"Hush, Rosalind." Lani flipped her hand at her and turned back to Sarah.

Seeing a small smile on Sarah's face was worth ignoring Rosalind's big mouth. Sometimes she forgot most people around here had never been to— nor seen— the ocean or a beach.

"Thanks for helping me," Sarah said softly. "The sorry . . . okay, at least we saved some hog-head cheese."

They all laughed a bit too hard, probably to lighten the mood. Then the nervously babbling girls helped dust the back of Lani's arms, also.

"Had to. Ye welcome," Lani said, scrunching up her nose. "Still, I no get used to all of the parts ya'll eat from the hog. Seems you eat everything 'cept the teeth. I, what's the word . . . crave, some fufu right now." She smacked her lips.

"Some, what?" Sarah asked.

"Ye, tez good. Cook cassava, like'a yams, let it thicken, then make dough balls." Lani grabbed at an imaginary ball and puckered her lips into a kiss.

Sarah grabbed her stomach and faked a gag. The girls all cackled. Then they headed inside, chatting about what they would do if the disgusting men came back, and all the cleaning up and repairing they'd have to help with tomorrow.

Behind them, Ben, Jeb, and other men were already swinging hammers and replacing the broken boards. She felt ready now to talk with Ben the very next chance she got. A dust cloud floated up the road leading to the house. It was a furious-looking Mr. Tate and his driver hurrying home. He leaped from the rolling wagon before the wheels stopped and sprinted inside.

CHAPTER FIFTEEN

At the breakfast gathering come morning, Felix had said, "Mas Tate was shole thankful Lani'd warned his wife. He knew 'zackly who those men were. And the sheriff's gone to get 'um.' Did it mean Lani got a break that Monday? No. However, she felt a bit more confident now moving throughout her days.

"Looka heah?" Miss Martha stood back and clasped her chest late the next Sunday afternoon. "Oh, I like your hair. I wuz wondin' if you'd take that old rag off," she announced to Lani, standing near the young folks gathered under a tree.

"Thanks. Nothing's going on around the cabin, so I got ready." Lani pulled at her loose-fitting dress and sighed. Her face felt warm as she looked down, embarrassed about her cabin mother complimenting her in front of a group. Even though it felt good hearing she dressed up pretty good. How she wished she could draw tiny white circles on the plain old dress, which would remind her of her tribe.

On the Saturday night before they'd had to move clothes, themselves, and pots and pans all over the floor to catch or miss the rain dripping through the leaking roof. Finally, this afternoon she'd found a clean, dry tan dress, thrown it on, and kinda strutted out to the gathering.

A few repaired cane bottom chairs were scattered underneath the trees. Miss Martha swiftly fanned herself with a black felt hat and was wearing a faded green dress and black shoes. Lani smiled at Miss Martha, who'd cocked her head to one side like she'd remembered an unpleasant memory. When Lani got closer, she saw a hint of anger in the woman's eyes.

Miss Martha opened and closed her fists, then glanced away from Lani and pointed at the fiddler. Her voice broke up. "I'll tell you. . . my sweetie, Felix . . . can play a fiddle. I can hardly wait. Massa gone let us get married and, 'jump the broom,'" she announced with a twinkle back in her eyes.

"Good . . . but, Miss Martha," Lani rolled her shoulders, and measured her words with kindness. "Why can't you share things from Africa like where you came from with the children or me?" For all the strict lady repeatedly told the young 'uns was—be thankful for the small things, thankful about today, the past was the past, and God was with us.

The motherly lady's face tightened. "Baby. Yes, I came to this plantation 'bout ten years ago, and sho remember my dear father sharing stories of village life and language from back home. Even the major initiation rites like the rite of birth, rite of adulthood, and rite of marriage, all which included lots of ceremonies and dancing," she said, pulling down hard on her hat and twisting it with a distant look in her eyes. "It's taken years for me to learn to block out painful memories . . . Now, I hope this new dreadful life, won't stop you from dreaming . . . It's getting late." Stepping over a mud puddle, she pranced over and sat next to Felix in an old chair.

Lani grunted, cleared her throat, and crossed her arms. "Miss Martha using big words? And a lot of *omugo*, stupid, nonsense talk," she mumbled and then slid closer in next to Margie.

After looking across at Mr. Felix and Miss Martha minutes later, however, she got tickled. Sometimes that couple reminded her of her mother and father. Felix's face was glowing while he gently bumped into Miss Martha as he played. He even had on a clean once-white shirt. She sure wished that one day the smart man would get to manage his own house and cotton fields.

Miss Martha peeked back at Lani strolling away with the girls. She leaned back like she wondered where Lani learned to walk with her head held high like that.

After about twenty minutes, Lani had to admit, a drumbeat on any soil was powerful. Once the high and low voices all blended in harmony with the instruments, she gradually dropped her arms. A few of the logs around her heart slowly chipped away with each thumpity thump. Soon, she rocked side to side with the tempo.

Thirsty, before long, she strolled away and sat down in a wet rope-bottom chair. She picked up a cup of water and closed her eyes for a minute. She was quite thankful she had a few hours of free time where an elder might tell one of those oral tales about smart rabbits and foxes, which were stories of victory for the weaker person. They made her feel hopeful, temporarily. The stories helped her push back dark, can't-do-nothing-about-it thoughts like remembering the capture. Or wondering which of her brothers maybe became a village chief back home. Perhaps several of her brothers were in this same country, too. Mainly, she pondered where and how her mother was doing.

When she opened her eyes, a grinning Sarah gave her an 'I told you' smile. Lani turned around curious as Ben came up behind her and rushed into a chair next to her. She crossed her ankles to keep them still.

"Heavenly woman, Lani," Ben's deep voice boomed out, and he gave her a mischievous grin.

Lani's head jerked back. Few people knew what her old name meant. They'd hardly spoken a word to each other. She felt utterly amazed he still remembered her African name. Not sure what to say or do, she felt delighted they were away from the crowd. She caressed her arms and watched him scoot his chair closer to hers.

"You remember naming ceremonies? What mine means?" She self-consciously reached up, smoothing her hair down.

"Sure. My other name was Agibe," he said as his eyes reddened. Then he glanced down, focusing on his shirt. He was glad he'd dug around and found one without holes this time. But most of all, he seemed excited to catch Lani alone away from her circle of girls, finally. He gazed deeply into her dark brown eyes.

"I got a cousin with that name. It means, tough," Lani declared and leaned away laughing. "And we gotta be tougher than tough, here."

He boastfully stuck out his chest. Together, they burst out laughing.

No matter how she'd avoided him, she had begun to like Ben's attention. Realizing he adored her was such a thrill. On the other hand, it'd be taking a chance on befriending and losing someone again. Their time together would be limited to only a few hours a week of free time.

On top of that, if Mr. Tate sold her, then what? She'd already heard that Mr. Tate told Ace to quit picking the mates for the girls when they turn fifteen 'cause he'd found out when the workers chose who they liked, they were less likely to run away.

"You forget? We from the same country. Different area. I know to run free, enjoy family. And . . ." He pulled up his pants leg. "See this." He pointed at a deep scar that went around his ankle. "That where they had me chained from one boat trip to the next. You, not the only one suffered heartache and pain." He balled up his fist and pounded them together.

Lani gave him a moment while she tried to think of what to say. "It seems to be healing well. Things are changing round here. Cotton bales stacking up in the barn. We planting and eating less. . . I . . . Well, we had some good festivals back home."

"Ye. Still, we both know. Neither of us lived in the king's hut, back in Africa. And it was a fight for survival." His voice lowered, and he touched her arm. She felt a quick flutter in her stomach. "We only got today, Lani . . . Lucy. And our minds are still free to dream."

She waved him off. "Please. We on the same level as mules. When will we get a chance to see our dreams? The slave that tried to run away at night last month, why they caught him trying to hide under cotton bales on a boat. They brought him back. Beat him, and charged an upset Mr. Tate for the catch," she huffed, angling her shoulder away from him.

Well, she'd finally got a close-up view of those thick bushy eyebrows, broad nose, and high forehead. Yes, Ben was nice looking. Still, she wondered why the fidgety fellow didn't cut his wild bushy crown of hair. It'd be disastrous to mention his scars, or how they could try to escape now. Even though Ben was one of the strongest older teenagers who always won in arm wrestling matches, so what? Would she let her heart get broken again?

"Heard from a neighbor's driver about this Civil War. Wonder why they call it civil? Anyway, there's a chance one day we can all be free. Not just in some states," he said, leaning into her side vision while smoothing down a fuzzy new mustache. He sensed her checking him out. They only had a few minutes with too much to forget or discuss. He sat back patiently.

"Free to do what? Go where? They hold us with fear. Here, and, outside of here. Please. That's *alekokoro*—crazy talk." Was it worth the risk—her life? She hopped up, straightened her dress, and started inside with the crowd before dark.

"Wait. Hold up." Ben signaled her to stop. "One side will win the war. I'm pulling for that President Lancon or Lincoln man's side. Maybe he or someone will help us be free. In the meantime, . . ." He cautiously stepped closer. "Next week at the dance . . . I want *you* to dance with *me*. Okay?" he said, stretching out his calloused hand to her.

Her hands felt damp from the water cup. Or something else? She reached back timidly to hold his hand while keeping a distance. He grabbed her hand and yanked her closer. His eyes lit up as their fingers intertwined, and she felt a warm jolt all over. Then they strolled shamelessly hand in hand across the sticky, muddy yard until they reached the lane in front of their cabins.

Oblivious at first to others when they floated past a group of girls, Lani did, however, catch a glimpse of Rosalind standing back with her arms folded sneering at them. She shrugged, waved at Ben, and went inside. How many times had Miss Martha told Rosalind to stop being so fast, always chasing boys? Just cause her dad was gone, she had to find peace within herself. She never imagined the jealous girl had chased after Ben, too.

Fluffing the pallet inside, did she dare dream of better days when as long as there was cotton in those fields, they'd try to hold her. Some slaves safely made it to freedom. She cringed inside thinking of how the men slaves here were picky about telling girls of their run-away plans. How did the escaped slaves get 'free' papers? Lani closed her eyes in deep consideration of the choices she had to make to get away.

Jamesa had said more slaves were running away to join the Union soldiers wanting to help fight in this war. One other piece of news she shared had her and all the slaves uneasy though. Several plantations were having to sell everything since the men owners were now away at war. Crops went unattended. Whole fields of peas dried up.

Even Mr. Tate, Felix found out, went back and forth over what he needed to sell off first—more gear, or workers? She had all that, and now Ben to think about before morning. Oh, but her dreams about Ben would be sweet dreams tonight.

CHAPTER SIXTEEN

It was a Wednesday afternoon and Lani was bent down with a bucket picking sweet peas. Today she had to help Miss Martha with canning in the hot, closed-in kitchen. The dread of feeling the extra heat from the roaring woodstove bothered her. Across the fence, she knew by his long strides Ace was patrolling the yard like a working ant. Darting here, rushing there. Mr. Tate seemed to be following right behind his overseer like he had something to tell him.

In this smaller garden nearest the kitchen were rows of onion plants budding with white flowers. Next to that were several rows of collards and turnip greens. Moaning, Lani hastily filled the tin bucket with peas. At the edge of the garden, a rabbit stood back a ways perched on its back legs like it hoped she'd leave him something to chew on.

She grinned, watching the rabbit quickly hop on across out into the tall weeds. A rabbit sure took a chance on his life running through this yard. "Smoked meat is a special meal around here," she whispered.

She rotated her aching neck. First, haul wood for the wood-stove. Then maybe ask the trusted cook to beg or borrow a few cloth scraps from the Missus. Even with the war going on, Missus Tate and her lady friends always dressed their best when they left their houses. So they needed dresses. The country was in a fight, and it raised high hopes for all people to have their rights heard. Why waste time dreaming about fairness? The freedom to buy and own things? She wished she could find her mother, or someone from her village.

After filling the bucket, she lifted it with two hands and headed towards the kitchen. "Anyone should know cooking should be done outside," she mumbled. After this, she had to help pull stinging weeds out of the cow pasture where there was little wind blowing. At least in the fields with the other young ladies, they could sneak and talk about boys, dances, and where were the closest towns and back roads.

Minutes later, a sweating Lani huffed through the open kitchen back door. Flies swarmed in and out throughout the kitchen. She sucked in air and dropped the heavy bucket down on the wooden table, picked up a dishrag nearby, and swatted at the flies. Miss Martha raised her eyebrows at her to 'watch it,' then pointed to a bowl for shelling peas. Without a head rag, Miss Martha's thick hair looked like black and gray cotton. Already her thin apron had sugar and flour stains all over it. She wiped her forehead wringing wet with sweat. After that, she turned her back and started just a banging and clanging pots onto the stove.

"I'm about tired of cooking for white folks," Miss Martha mumbled.

"Ma'am?"

The usually obedient lady complained and kept grumbling to herself without answering Lani. She wanted to ask again what she said, but decided against upsetting the chief cook today. For when Miss Martha wanted to, she could mess up some food. Leave the salt out. Burn the bottom of the bread.

The pleasant smell of cinnamon floated over the kitchen as Lani wondered what dish baked in the oven. She pulled out a basket for the pea hulls. A cold drink would be refreshing now. If only they had a spot other than the water well to keep things cool. She grabbed a wooden chair from the table, pulled it close to the one open window on the right, hoping for any breeze.

Then she heard deep voices outside coming near the window. So she scooted up, alarmed, and tried recognizing who was talking. With the bowl in her lap, she peered outside, straining to hear. Lanky Ace and Mr. Tate were right in each other's faces.

"Eh, Ace. With the bad drought of last year, and the war going on? Also, with my boys being off in a war regiment, I got to sell a few things, cut some costs. We're struggling . . . I'm a have to let you go," Mr. Tate said with a stern voice.

Lani made a whistling sound and signaled with her head for Miss Martha to stop stirring in the pots and come closer. Miss Martha gave her an eye like, 'mind your own business, child.'

However, curious too, she crept over and they eavesdropped from either side of the window. Cautiously, Lani tilted herself more into the window frame getting a better angle of them, yet stayed out of their sight.

"Well. You can bet this sorry farm will go to pieces without me." Ace was spitting when he talked, and his eyes narrowed. "Ima skedaddle away from here as fast as possible. Then Ima find me any kinda paying job with the Confederate gov'ment. We gotta protect our rights. I got a family to take care of." He threw his raggedy whip at Mr. Tate, backed up a few steps, and made a choking sign at him.

Mr. Tate lunged after Ace, but with his short arms he swung only at air. At once, Ace spun around and tramped off towards the horse barn. Then Mr. Tate stopped short and started scratching his beard up and down for several seconds. Lani wondered if he was in deep thought or a mosquito bit him?

Both kitchen workers immediately resumed their duties as the frustrated man passed by the window grumbling to himself. When he got to the front of the house, they moved in slow motion absorbing the new fact. Ace going was the best news she had heard all year. She put the bowl down, slapped her chest, then did a rocking dance in the chair.

Miss Martha loosened her apron strings, raised her hands, and bent into a holy dance mouthing, "Thank you, Lord. Thank ye. A little break."

As Lani chuckled, she mulled over the notion of a paying job. Could she get paid for working? Making quilts and dyeing fabric to sell? Oh, what she could do with a little money.

"*Ki ni*—what? What?" Lani chanted while dumping peas into a bowl. "Miss Martha, what if you got paid for cooking, me for sewing? Maybe buy our freedom. I'd buy myself a real bed, some pretty cloth, or save up enough to catch a ship back home. That'd be nice."

"Hush, now. Focus on helping me prepare this supper." Miss Martha actually started grinning, with a dreamy expression, too.

Soon the kitchen overflowed with more aromas of clove and vanilla spices mixed with a buttery smell. Peach cobbler. Lani planned to taste at least one corner of it. At evening time, peopled mulled around bone-tired and sweaty. The yard gossip started. Who would replace Ace? Who else might get sold? This might be a safer time to escape. She wanted to get with the girls and talk before dark, but she had to help Miss Martha clean up after supper.

An hour later, she slung dirty, murky dishwater around and planned to sneak out tonight and talk with Ben, if there was a full moon. If he got sold, how would she find him? Miss Martha glanced at her with her apron wet and stained with food spots and dumped the dishwater out to the chickens.

"Now, wrap us a piece of bread for Sam'l, and Wil'm, so they won't whine so at night," Miss Martha directed, putting up the last pan.

"Why I got to always save them something? What about Lettie Mae or Margie helping watch out for the boys, too?"

"Cause wez a family in our cabin. And they don't get much rations. All our stomachs are growling, and flapping empty at night these days."

Lani banged the wooden spoon against the table and clenched her jaws while scraping the corner of two pans getting the last of the cornbread. With her mother being somewhere else, it seemed everybody tried being her boss. The lazy-eyed lady would holler at her for being out past bedtime. House boss, Missus Tate, decided who worked where. Plus, Miss Martha watched over them like a soaring hawk.

"If only I could talk with Missus about how we could sell pretty cloth," she mumbled. "Right before dark, I must speak with the girls about getting away from here."

With Ace gone, less food, and a busy Mr. Tate running from one field to the other looking worried, things were changing. Stuffing two biscuits into her pocket, she hurried outside and waved at Ben. He sat on the ground leaning back on his arms and staring off into space. He looked beyond worn out. Finally noticing her, he smiled widely, waved back, then fell backward like a dead tree—fast asleep.

On a Monday morning two weeks later, Mr. Tate appeared exhausted while standing on the garret or porch. He looked like he'd wrestled all night with his problems. The workers gathered in front of him, fidgeting around, a bit surprised. An early morning meeting was unusual. He took off his dusty hat, then put it back on. Lani gazed past the house, and her head started hurting as she imagined the worst. The month of May had spread green plants like a blanket all around them. On the right side, out by the stable, the grass glistened like sparkles covered with the morning dew.

Up front, Tate's loud voice boomed over the workers. "My brother, Mack, wrote me, and I'm taking a few workers down to help him. And he'll help me get more supplies. The Union army's trying to block folks from selling our cotton up north. And so, we're gonna try and sell bales to Mexico." He peered to his right out over the much smaller fields and then back at the confused workers.

"Only a few of my best workers will go," he continued like he was talking to himself. "Both ... of my sons ... are in the war ..." He seemed to get choked up, swallowed hard, then adjusted his stance, and said, "My wife will handle the house till I get back. And Felix's got the rest. I don't care about a law which says I can't leave a slave in charge. This is my property. Remember, the patty rollers are still catching runaways. Go by the table over there to see where you go." He fanned his hands out for dismissal.

Somebody standing nearby groaned and said, "Oh Lord, Felix is the devil's brother, with no sympathy."

There was a lot of mumbling and questioning expressions. Lani grunted as the group dispersed to a table where the Missus sat writing. *What's going on this time?* The line moved fast since

153

they'd already made out a list, as if they only had to decide which animals went where. She felt numb as she approached the table.

From biting dogs, patty rollers, a beating, to guns were the high, imaginary fences that surrounded them and prevented them from escaping. Lani stepped up next in line.

Swiftly, Missus Tate told her she was going to Mack's plantation. Where? She frowned and poked along to chop weeds. Then Ben ran up behind her and pushed her gently.

"You heard? I'm being hired out." He matched her stride as they went to the field. "Ye. On one of the neighbor's farms. The wife's abandoned since her husband's in the army. I wish I could go fight with the Union soldiers," he said wistfully. Then he dropped his arms straight down and began marching in a military-drill style alongside her.

She laughed to relieve the tightness in her throat. "You might get hurt. And I'd be wondering where you were," she said with concern and touched him to stop.

Ben paused and blinked as if suddenly relieved. "I'll wait for you to get back . . . So, you *care* if I get hurt?" He leaned back, watching her stammer, wordless. "I'll be careful cause I want to get back hea and hang around you. . . till wez free." He gazed into her sparkling eyes, pumped a fist to his chest, backed up, then ran off to harness the mules.

Lani covered her open mouth and tingled all over. Then, she stepped lightly through the moist grass on the way to the fields. Her feet and dress tail were covered in scratchy dirt mixed with the wet dew. Miss Martha and Sarah had been told they would stay at the farm to make lye soap. At least she 'sort of' had a reason to want to return to this unbearable place. Even still, she worried about what might be on the other plantation.

Should she run away and risk being caught, beat, lynched, or molested? Or keep hoping this war between the tribes or states could one day free her? Which freedom should she prepare for? When she entered the kitchen after supper, Miss Martha stood in a corner tying up something in a bundle. The upcoming trip had her focused on what to carry from the kitchen. "Heah, I wrapped you up some dried meat. And . . ." She handed Lani another tied rag. "Run and put these fabric scraps on yo' bed. I got 'em from the trash," she said with a 'you deserve it' smile.

Lani quickly flung her arms around Miss Martha's neck.

"Listen." Miss Martha gently pushed Lani back and gazed directly into her eyes. "I had Jamesa show Missus Giruth one of the blocks you made. More and more plantation owners ez hiring out special type work. Now the Tates know the ones that get paid gone do their best work. She wants you to come up to the big house, before dark." Miss Martha's face seemed hopeful for one of her children. "And, she said Miss Giruth's checking into having cloth sent here. So perhaps you can get something for making pretty dresses or shirts. She still 'member you warning her."

"No. Oh my, money?" Lani didn't quite believe this even though a visiting driver had told them about a freed slave who worked as a bootmaker in the next town. Maybe. Miss Martha had no reason to make this up. She knew talented dressmakers were needed. And she liked imagining what a couple of yards of cloth could become. Lani looked uncertainly towards the big house.

"Yep. They let the person needing the help pay the slaves something. After they pay Mr. Tate. Sho nuff, they already hired out Osaze, or Owen, as a hide tanner in town. Also, Ben and Jeb—"

Lani backed out the door in a daze, down one block step, pivoted, and marched toward the cabin with one rag swinging in her left hand, and one in the right. She wanted to dream, but had been disappointed so many times before. Not being included in any 'men's only' runaway plans had upset her. However, this chance to finally use the drawings in her mind could be the start to freedom.

When the sunlight faded across the yard, Lani picked up an egg wire basket and moseyed towards a door of the big house again.

CHAPTER SEVENTEEN

Most of the workers were lying out in their front yards staring off into space or sleeping. The setting evening sun filtered through the thick trees. Lani wanted it to look like she was picking up extra eggs for breakfast. But the truth was, if they knew she was summoned to the big house there'd be too many questions. Was she in trouble? Maybe there was a late mess she had to help clean up?

She waved to a few people sitting in the doorway of the last shack and trotted faster. Remembering the previous time she had knocked on the door, she softly climbed the three steps and tapped on it timidly. Jamesa cracked the back door, peeking out. The heavenly smell of freshly baked bread drifted out, and Lani so wanted to ask for a piece.

"It's late. What do you want?" Jamesa snapped with her apron that was usually clean and white, but now it was filled with brown smudges. Her expression showed she'd had a full day and was tired.

"Miss Martha said Missus Giruth wants to see me today," Lani said, shifting her feet.

Jamesa knew it must be true for the girl to come up here unless she'd been requested. She nodded to Lani and slammed the door. Just left Lani standing there wondering how she could talk to Miss Giruth directly. Before today, she'd only stood, taken orders, then obeyed Mr. or Missus Tate. Pounding footsteps over the wooden floor were coming her way. Louder. Dropping her head and clearing her throat several times, Lani waited. Should she back up, run? When the doorknob turned, she immediately gazed down and took a step back, holding her breath. Missus stepped out.

"Lucy. I saw one of the quilt layouts you helped Martha and the others finish. I believe you could be a custom seamstress," Missus Giruth got right to the matter she'd call the girl for.

Lani slowly raised her head, catching the gentle look on the lady's face. She said nothing. Missus Giruth was wearing a button-up beige blouse with a long flowing brown skirt. She leaned down further as if ready to repeat what she'd said.

"Yes'um. But what is a seamtrus, ma'am?" Lani frowned, rolling her fingers.

Missus Giruth chuckled. "Well, you will sew custom clothes for folks." She gazed out over the porch. "A few days ago we could've lost it all."

Lani's gaze met hers, then dropped. She had forgotten not to look the woman in the eye.

"Mas Tate and I have decided to hire out more workers, allow some even to buy their freedom."

Lani stiffened. Was the lady fooling her? She told herself to ask, hire out where? How much am I worth? But instead said, "Ma'am, eh, I can draw 'em out in the dirt first, then cut the cloth pieces, then, about how much can I make?" She hated it when she got nervous when speaking because she talked too fast and chopped her words. That meant whoever was listening strained to understand her.

Missus Tate swallowed hard, looking past Lani like she knew to get her best work, she would let the customers pay a few greenbacks to the talented girl. It had been a weighted decision for them. "You sew. We'll work it out for you to get paid. Get some rest. You've got a long trip soon."

Humph, blinking hard, Lani realized the possibility of buying her freedom was more than she ever expected. The Tates would get extra money, and a few workers could earn a little money, too. Maybe. She stared at Miss Giruth's dress and felt the lady watching her. Both were standing there thinking, waiting for Lani to respond.

"Thank you," was all she could mumble. But she felt anger boiling inside that was about to spill over into a crazy laugh. Because she figured she'd do all the work, but would the customers give her anything? Lani heard the screen door slam as Miss Giruth went inside. She grunted. Guess there is some good, deep down in most folks. Like her father'd say, "Sometimes you have to search for the deep parts of the river to catch the biggest fish."

It is like her legs were stuck to the porch, as she kept thinking. Yes, she'd noticed that the Tates were now forced to find other ways to save the plantation by sending their workers out to other farms.

Was it better to be free and worry about your next meal, or a slave with at least one meal coming? Free. She knew how to eat things grown in the wild. After Jeb had shown his money to a few workers, she felt that whether she was paid now, or after freedom, at least she'd know a trade.

Quietly she tiptoed over to the high back chair on the right. Something she always wanted to do. Just like the Missus. Sit in that rocking chair, doing nothing but a 'rocking. She eased down while watching the back door, and back and forth she went. Oh, to sew like her mother. When other ladies in their village needed a new dress, often, Toluwani would tell them to raise their arms, and she'd measure them. Before long, the expectant ladies would come back and pick up a dress perfect for their body. Big hips, thin waists, and all.

After only a few seconds, abruptly a voice down the lane yelled something about "get back here." Startled, she hopped up smiling and ran back to the quarters trying not to worry about the upcoming work trip. Visions of ruffles and dresses she'd admired on some of Missus Giruth's lady friends kept flashing through her mind. Should she tell the girls about this talk with the Missus or keep it a secret? Scanning the yard, she looked for an old syrup bucket, just in case she needed to store some money.

They did not leave for the other plantation yet, and it had been a grueling two weeks to finish a church dress for the mayor's wife. The satisfied lady had twirled several times admiring herself in that new dress. Lani remembered stepping outside afterward, slyly pulling from her pocket a wad of two greenbacks that the mayor's wife had given her. She'd stared at the paper bills front and back, feeling it between her fingers. Then she anxiously ran and tore a hole in her pallet and stuffed the money deep inside.

On a Wednesday the next week, a high wave of joy still flooded her. But it faded somewhat to a low tide of despair when she thought of how long it might take to buy her freedom. How long could she hold on to that faraway dream? She shrugged her shoulders—just like collecting straw for a basket, what she had was a start. If folks could just be given a chance to make it.

At suppertime, instead of taking the risk of being snubbed again by the girls, just because she now worked inside. Lani ambled over toward a seat by herself. When she spotted Sarah sprawled out on her back under a different tree, she swiftly changed her mind. She'd take a chance that Sarah would not get up and move away.

On several rows out to the right were red and green tomatoes still clinging to the vines. Under a small shed, a group of workers was finishing up culling the rotten tomatoes from the good ones. Most of the other workers were eating their food quietly.

"Sarah, the mayor's wife was talking yesterday something about conductors helping slaves escape. And folks were mad about that." Lani sat down cautiously on the hard ground with a bowl of bean licker and cornbread. She stretched and closed her aching hands, while watching Sarah glare at her with an impatient look.

"Conductors, what?" Sarah covered her eyes with both hands. "Since you've been sewing up in the big house, you forget how worn out we are?"

"Please. You know I've been working just as hard. Try sewing with three sets of eyes watching you: Missus Giruth, Jamesa, and a dress customer all circling you threading a needle . . . Even when I finished, I know it was worth more for all that work." Lani puckered her lips, noticing the tomato juice and seeds stains on Sarah's dress.

Gently Sarah sat up, scraped at the seeds, and said nothing.

"Anyway, a conductor is a person that helps slaves know which houses and routes to safely get to a free state."

Sarah's face lit up with interest, and she stopped chewing. "We need to find a way to meet one."

Lani nodded and finished her supper. She certainly knew several workers were mumbling behind her back things like, "Lani thinks she's something now that she's not sweating like us." Snappy Rosalind and the other girls would move to a different tree when she came near them at eating time. But if they only knew how she nervously worried about getting slapped for sticking the lady with a pin. Or if she had measured correctly? Either way, she decided the girls needed to meet tonight for planning.

Then Sarah stiffly got up leaving, and Lani followed her into the lane.

"Boo." A husky-voiced Margie dashed at them from the corner of a cabin.

"Girl, you scared us," Lani said, holding her hand back for them all to stop, while she calmed down. "Listen, even if we get greenbacks or money to buy our freedom, we probably want to pay someone to take us away from here. Who will hire us in town?"

"Shoot, Mas Tate's subject to let some buy their freedom. Then sell the rest of us, and head back to Georgia, okay," Sarah said, gazing forward. "Some of my folks are there. But I won't get my hopes up."

"*Otito*, true. Ya'll know, we need to find out who the freed slaves are with the passes in town. They will tell us who the conductors are. It can be done." Lani put a commanding tone into her voice.

Sarah and Margie folded their arms and gave her a maybe-so look.

With their full attention, Lani continued, "One African saying I remember is: "birth does not differ from birth, as the free man is born, so is the slave.""

Sarah leaned her head into her hand. "Never heard of that in my life."

"Well, once free, we'll figure it out. That Harriet Tubman lady did it. We can, too," Lani said, thinking of how her father came back from hunting trips explaining how they'd kept from getting lost. What to look for in the forest to guide them on the way back home.

"Still," Sarah added, "the only time we can sneak off is at night. What if I find something to do, to get hired out, too? A paid mid-wife or, a root doctor. I can help sick people." She placed one hand on her hip and seemed to ponder her choices.

Gradually, more adults started passing around them going inside, and Sarah kept standing there, twirling one of her long braids.

Walking on, Lani turned to Margie. "When I go to Mas Tate's brother's place, I'll listen for how they getting those cotton bales to Mexico," she said, glad the girls were talking again with plans of how to escape.

"Yes, it's gotta be people riding with the cotton. And since you're getting the latest news, like Jamesa, the other girls will come around," Margie announced, slapping Lani on the back and strolling inside.

Lani almost fell over. When she straightened up, she reminded herself that if they needed to fight someone away from here, Margie was ready. She shuffled to their front door.

"What are you going to do, Lani? Come inside, or stand there looking crazy?" Wil'm blurted out, standing in the door frame with his head tilted.

Her vision came back into focus. The mischievous boy's tangled hair had knots rolled into it. She reached over and caught her finger in his thick hair, trying to detangle it. Wil'm hollered, ducked back, and twisted away.

In the house after dark was one rule. Add to that, everyone wondered who to trust. Who was the Massa's spy? Someone who'd try to get in favor with Massa and tell on a disobedient worker. Like who stole extra food from the crib, or who was planning something. Anything to get a pass to go to town or another favor Massa may give them. With all this to watch for, before the girls worked out how to get to the local shipping port, the covered wagon was loaded down at daybreak on a Tuesday morning.

Five workers, crock water jugs, and croaker sacks full of dried corn and beans were loaded ready to go to another plantation. Hooked to the wagon were two restless, grayish horses swishing their tails to fan flies away. Lani waited patiently on the second bench, gnawing her lip.

In the backyard, some workers were sleepwalking from their shacks towards the main house. The jersey cow dragged along toward the milk barn on the west side of the house where her calf and the milkers waited. Then Mr. Tate hopped up front, reached down, and put his bag under his seat.

All of a sudden, Sam'l came running over, waving a piece of paper in his hand.

"Hold it. Missus say Lucy has the wrong pass," he gasped, almost out of breath when he reached the wagon. He handed it up to Mr. Tate and bent down coughing.

Mr. Tate studied the paper, then turned around. "Lucy, let me see what you have."

Lani twitched. Confused, she reached into her pocket, retrieved her pass, and handed it to him.

"Here, see this L-U-C-Y. That's yours." He pointed to the writing on the other paper. "This one's for Lettie." He took hers, reached back and gave Lettie Mae the other one.

Lettie Mae stuffed it into her pocket. As Lani sat back on her seat, she ran her fingers over the spelling of her name, touching each letter slowly. One day, she hoped to learn how to write her own name.

When Mr. Tate popped the whip, the horses reared up, and the loaded wagon rolled out onto the road. Lani fidgeted with her dress and felt trapped in a tight space on her bench. They rocked along in silence, bouncing side to side down the rough road. She squeezed her forehead forward, then back. Ow wee, her scalp hurt. Lettie Mae had pulled and plaited her hair last night. And since her hair was shorter in the back, it felt like someone was pulling her brain through her scalp.

Thinking about getting relief for her head helped her forget about the other worries about this trip. Same work, different location. Either way, she was determined to stay true to her mother's words, "we're the survivors."

Gazing behind them at the workers going to the outdoor table for breakfast, she felt better knowing the untiring Rosalind had finally found a boyfriend that liked her, Jeb, the funny, good-hearted fellow that most of the other girls had rejected. After some consideration, she agreed they made a good couple. Even better, Mr. Tate had said they'd pick up Ben from the neighbor's farm on their way back. That was good. However, she planned to make notes in her head of roads, houses, and land markers away from here.

The wagon hit potholes and deep ruts, swaying the riders while they traveled through the countryside filled with yellow wildflowers and scattered plantations. Like an unexpected arrow, suddenly, her spirits leaped with hope remembering Mr. Tate's brother had bought Molayo and Fadila. She could only pray they were still there.

CHAPTER EIGHTEEN

After riding for hours on a broader road until dust dark, thankfully, Mr. Tate decided they'd rest a while and start back up in the morning. They pulled off the roadway into a clearing near a flowing creek that gurgled over large rocks. After Lani jumped down and stretched her legs, she eased up close to the horses. The thirsty horses slurped loudly from the muddy branch water as she splashed refreshing water on her face and hair. Then she went to find a flat area to rest.

Next thing she heard frogs croaking and then a crunching movement sound in the woods.

Behind her she could see the glow of a low campfire Mr. Tate'd built, so she hurried back near the others. As the rustling sounds appeared to come closer, she and the others huddled nearer to the fire, peering out into the woods. Lani cleared her throat to stop a nervous tickle. Maybe it was a wild animal, or a slave captor. More crunching sounds. She almost giggled while she studied where to run, when and if something began an attack.

The horses were moving, restless, neighing, and pulling against their tied ropes. Louder movements. Closer. From his mat, a fumbling Mr. Tate jumped up and reached into the wagon beside him.

Threateningly the man stood flatfooted and shouted out into the woods, "Okay, who's there? Don't come any closer." He cocked the rifle and pointed out into the darkness.

By that time, all the workers were right upon each other, holding hands. Whatever was approaching them, it was more than one person or animal. The noises were coming from different angles. Her eardrums pounded with the rapid beat of her racing heartbeat. Where could she hide? Under a quilt in the wagon or dash into the darkness, hoping to find the road? She braced to bolt, but the others held her tight like a lock on a gate. Thankfully, the full moon provided some night vision, but she could not see past the thicket surrounding them.

Finally, after a couple of minutes, a man shouted, "Hey, don't shoot. It's us—just a band of Confederate soldiers. We're on our way back to camp. Gun down, sir. We've had Union soldier spies passing through here, and we don't want to hurt anybody else."

In a ready-for-action pose, Mr. Tate explained he had passes for all his slaves, and he was just going to his brother's plantation.

By this time, Lani had squeezed her eyes shut and start singing softly, "*Gba pada buburu, gba pada buburu.*"

All heads turned towards her.

Lettie Mae whispered in her ear, "What, song? Sing it again. I . . . know it," she said uncertainly.

"Means, get back, evil. *Gba pada buburu*."

Lettie Mae giggled nervously and joined in. Then the next lady did, followed by all the others around the campfire who soon caught the tune and sang along.

The rustling in the thicket ceased. At any moment, she tensed, believing they'd grab her and take her away. Again. Thankfully, soon only the sounds of night crickets and owls hooting echoed throughout the woods. Opening her eyes one at a time, she glimpsed a line of men marching away. The faint sound of, "left, left, left right, left," echoed through the woods.

They hadn't come to capture her? She fell back flat on the ground and blew out wind from both ends of her body. She felt Toluwani would've been proud of her. For she neither laughed nor cried this time. Just breathed in, breathed out. Oh my, she squeezed her eyes tightly, *Well, walking on hot coals, or eating bitter food, is nothing compared to the hardships of surviving in this country.*

Mr. Tate told them to get some rest. They were leaving this area early in the morning. He assured them that everything was okay. However, an hour later, he nor anyone else could sleep. It was then that Lani felt she'd never see her mother again. She was on her own. Yet somehow, they would both survive.

With the full moon in their favor, after about thirty more minutes he directed them to load back up. Some workers leaped up clapping while Lani and the others popped up like popcorn and hurriedly threw their belongings on the buckboard. Then they attached a lit lantern to the side of the wagon.

"Mack's farm here we come," Lani mouthed. They were getting out of there immediately.

Arriving mid-morning the next day, the horses trotted faster when they turned onto the road leading to Mr. Mack Tate's big farm. Anxiously, Lani peered ahead, repeatedly tightening and loosening her head rag. Maybe, just maybe, Molayo would still be on Mack's plantation.

Even before they stopped, both sides of the road were draped with a sea of white flowering cotton stalks that flowed to eternity. Near the roadway, there was a field of corn with its tassels and silks swaying in the wind. The horse and buggy bounced and rocked past several small cabins with open doors. An old lady waved as they passed by as Lani gazed around at the cabins, searching for a familiar face.

On the right were several workers out hoeing and chopping yet another cotton field. They had on their long-sleeved shirts and raggedy hats. She groaned, thinking of the endless work and long, long, rows.

In the distance where the road ended, she could not believe it. Mr. Tate said "whoa" in front of a two-story mansion with a balcony on the top floor with a full-length porch on the first floor. The house was a starch white color with black shutters adorning large windows, complete with two large columns with wide pedestals. Scanning the yard, her eyes bucked. Green grass covered the front yard instead of everyday dirt that someone needed to rake.

Why her whole village could have shared Mr. Mack's *titobi*, huge house, she uttered to herself and kept hoping to recognize someone.

"My, this country has endless riches," she whispered to Lettie Mae. "One day, I will have a house, a farm, too."

"Me too," Lettie said, checking left and right beyond the waiting horses. Her eyes looked dreamy. "Oh, I see lots of heads of hair I can fix around here . . . but look."

A fancy black carriage with large red wheels and two white horses with red tassels in their manes rolled up in front of them. A worker ran out of the fields and helped a tight-walking Mr. Tate get his bags into the showy carriage which would carry him to the main house. The driver of the carriage sat up front, dressed in a tall black hat with a matching black suit, white gloves, and his coat tail dangled below the seat. Lani stared hard at him, twice, and just knew his arms hurt because he hadn't moved an inch while holding the reins up with stiff arms.

Within seconds, the workers slid down off the wagon. She squinted to the field past the house where workers toiled. She focused in on one lady. Just by the way she tilted her head, yes, yes, she knew it was Molayo. Lani rocked side to side, trying to contain her excitement and waited for directions. To her disappointment, they were handed a drink of water, given hoes and rakes, and pointed to the fields. Still, Lani ran almost breathlessly, stopping as close as possible to Molayo's row.

Supporting herself on a hoe, Molayo stood straight up in total disbelief with her mouth gaped. And three rows over, Fadila abruptly stopped chopping, too, gazing at Lani. The girls realized quitting work to greet each other could cause a lashing. But a defiant Molayo dropped her hoe and started jumping up and down.

Lani bent forward and then back up, squeezing her lips to keep from bursting. Straight to work she went, yet this time, she worked with more purpose. Break time.

So, all three girls were together again working, surviving, and adjusting to their new country, language, altered lives, and remarkably much more. After a lot of sweating and sore hands on this hot June day, by mid-day the workers were allowed an afternoon break. Still a leader, Molayo motioned for Lani and a few other young people to follow her.

Almost running, she led them down an old Indian trail toward a clearing. Once protected by the tall trees from the overseer's watch, Lani and a more relaxed Molayo joined hands and started spinning in circles, bouncing on their toes. Lani winced because of the raw, sore spots between her thumb and forefinger from chopping all that cotton. Just like a bubbling spring, their tears began to overflow.

After a few minutes of hugging and spinning, Lani finally said. "How've you been? Who's the fellow that held your hand?

Oh, I like that bracelet. What's your new name?" The questions rolled out.

Molayo's high cheeks had such a glow. She felt good all over witnessing a small smile on Molayo's face for the first time since she'd known her.

"Mariah," the new Molayo stepped back and tapped under her eyes, realizing break time was short. "But I'll always be Molayo. We find a way to move forward." Holding up her wrist she said, "Look, I made these bracelets from dried acorns and rope. Come on. I've gotta show you something at the river," she yelled, swinging her arms and racing ahead.

When Lani looked back, she spotted Fadila coming in the group behind them. She now had fuller hips and still glided like royalty entering the room. Hesitant at first, she gave Fadila a quick smile. Luckily, Fadila returned it with a big smile while lifting different cloths from her pocket. Lani braced herself, squeezing her hands together as she waited to see what Fadila had. She approached her with outstretched arms, and both girls embraced in a long hug.

Stepping back, she asked Fadila, "What you got in your pocket this time?" Memories of their ship experiences flooded her mind.

Fadila laughed. Then she yanked her dirty white head rag off, replacing it with a purple velvet headband which she tied around her forehead, like a crown. "See what I've made from what Missus Mack Tate's seamstress gave me." Fadila pulled out two more velvet headbands. One was black, edged with gold ribbon, and the other one red trimmed in a fancy beige lace. "Uh, my new name is, Eli-za-beth."

Lani raised her palms for a high hand tap. "Oh, I like it. Just like a queen."

They tapped palms.

"*Beeni,* yes, I just know it. One day you will find a way to write to your father, and, he *will* pay for someone to bring you back. Or come himself."

Fadila pursed her lips like 'and you know it.'

Lani beamed all over while sprinting to catch up with that fast Molayo who'd disappeared down the trail into a thicket. That is when she saw it. She stopped and absorbed the view. Oh, my goodness! Pure white silt sand lined a wide flowing river, right in the middle of Texas. A river beach. She shuffled back like a prancing horse while slapping her legs, utterly speechless.

Mischievously, Molayo gazed back at her with a wide grin. "Yep." She pointed to the sand. "Also, one of Mr. Mack's workers ran away to join the Union army. As you know, there's a war going on and one day we may be *free*. Free to sell our bracelets, or be what we want to be. If not us, then maybe our children, and—"

Molayo stopped, then she wrapped both arms around her waist and rocked. Staring directly into Lani's surprised eyes, she dropped her hands and said, "Also . . . someone told me they know where Miss Toluwani is, and she's the 'head nurse' on the place. And she sent word if someone sees her daughter, can they tell her, *kaabo ni*, welcome?" She clenched her lips, watching Lani.

"Wait. Moeder?" Lani's body froze in motion.

The news of her mother caused her heart to almost stop. She shook her head to make sure she was awake. *Kaabo ni?* Yes, it dawned on her that welcome-in was the final step in the passage ceremony before the dance.

If the girls did not quit from their separation from others, hard, painful tests, they would be welcomed in, and then learn the dance steps. Stronger. Feeling more self-confident now as a woman filled with self-worth. Rolling her shoulders, she breathed deeply, then with both hands picked up some white sand and let it trickle through her fingers, smiling.

"Also," Molayo paused with all now listening, "another worker said there's a new town back home called Freetown, and former slaves are catching a ship to go back there."

Lani pushed up the sleeves on her dress. Then she put her hands on her hips. "I'll tell you this. Forget getting on another ship. Even with this no-fair life, there's way too much water between here and back home." She gestured up and down the river beach.

"With the union and rebel soldiers fighting here and up North? One day *esan*, or for sure, one way or the other, we'll be free. Have *us* a hut filled with a family. We earn money. Right here, in this country." She raised her head and showed all of her teeth, buck teeth and all. "*Onise Nla*, great God, we're gonna make it," she declared.

Then she began skipping and kicking up sand and smiling and twirling around until falling on her side. She decided her life back across the ocean was gone. She would survive with her faith and guidance by elders like Miss Martha. So hopping back up, she dusted off her hands, and then quickly raised her knee, signaling Molayo. Someone struck up a hand-clap beat.

Even though Lani and the other workers had to continue to work as slaves, there were slaves who made it to freedom, and she felt she would survive until she was free.

Before she left the river beach, Lani, now known as Lucy, made sure she learned the grand ending steps of the passage dance on the new white sand. Mostly, she realized she could still love and dream.

Epilogue

S ome slaves made it to freedom through the underground railroad to Mexico, up north to free states, bought their freedom, or were granted independence in a master's will.

In the fall of 1862, Ben did escape while hired out to haul a neighbor's crop into town. He ran off to join a Colored Infantry in Louisiana. Lani never saw him again, but felt he made it. She imagined him high stepping as he wore a navy blue jacket, with shiny brass buttons, in a drill with other Union Colored soldiers. And that Sarah became a root doctor, teaching people how to use herbs and roots for their healing.

A presidential proclamation and executive order issued September 2, 1862, by President Abraham Lincoln, and effective January 1, 1863, emancipated the slaves. It was over two years later, however, for Lani and the Texas slaves who were finally freed on June 19th, 1865. After the Tates freed their slaves, they decided to stay in the area and built a branch of his father's corn grist mills. The mill became the largest one in the county.

The first thing Lani did after being freed was to find someone to write to the plantation where Toluwani was previously enslaved. After her mother was located, she saved enough money to visit Toluwani, who was down there pounding black walnut hulls for sick folks. They stayed in touch through the mail until her mother passed. Lani not only became a paid seamstress, but became highly sought after for the special dyed effects and designs she added to the fabric. She went on to have children, grandchildren, and great-grandchildren who would appreciate their worth, and one day own property while becoming productive, paid citizens of North America.

Many slaves came from the same African countries, but each region in that country used different dialects of Yoruba or their native language. With her new name, Lucy, along with other former slaves, they had to decide after their freedom, how they would continue to endure and live on. Paid skilled laborers such as blacksmiths, custom seamstresses,tailors, weavers, and others were an essential part of the American economy back then to offset low cotton sales.

Some freedmen chose the tenant farmer method, which is where the owners lived in town and allowed the farmers to live on and work their farm with little or no supervision. They sold what they could for money. While other freedmen chose the sharecropper method where they received a simple house, and monthly cash advances to tide the family over until the end of the crop season. After they sold their crops, they had to pay their landlords back.

Which method did they choose, how did they adjust to their new freedom, and did they stay on the same farms as paid workers, or leave? They all had to decide.

By 1874, former slaves did purchase land on or near plantations where they previously were considered property. This data was researched and verified by their location during the 1870 and 1880 US census. In some areas of Texas and throughout the United States, the land they bought is still being managed and used by family members today.

They, like us, must learn to persevere, plan, and dream using our creative minds to make where we land, a better place.

Discussion Questions

1. Which characters did you most identify with and why?

2. Did you have a person who acted as a surrogate mother to you? How?

3. Do you think Lani made the best choice, when she was alone in the woods? Why? What may have happened if she'd chose differently?

4. Have you ever had to make a difficult decision to stay or leave a location, relationship, or other situation?

5. What role did her father play in Lani's life? How can a distant parent still nurture or influence their children?

6. Were you surprised by the way the Tates treated their slaves? Why?

7. Some slaves escaped on an underground railroad to Mexico? What is your response to that?

8. What were some of the disadvantages for both races living during the 1859-1862 time period?

9. The discussion of American slavery in the past is often uncomfortable. What is your response to the relevance of a teenage slave story today?